Felix Publishing 2020
email: info.felixpublishing@gmail.com
Print copies available from publisher.

The Innocence of Tom Shipley, Teacher

2020 digital book release
ISBN: 978-1-925662-23-8
Print Edition
ISBN: 978-1-925662-22-1
Author: Dr. Peter T. Scott

Registration:
Thorpe-Bowker +61 3 8517 8342
email: bowkerlink@thorpe.com.au

The Innocence
of
Tom Shipley: Teacher.

Peter T. Scott

First released 2020

To the hard-working members of the
teaching fraternity worldwide

This book is a work of fiction. Any resemblance to people living
or dead is purely coincidental. Some characters may be a blend
of several personalities and multiple locations over many years.
Incidents as described in this book do happen in schools.

Contents

Chapter One: In the Beginning

Wow! I had made it! I was a teacher at last on my First Appointment! This was my first thought as I sat back in the seat of my Second-Class rail carriage of the National Capital Express heading south to Canberra, the capital city of Australia. Well... 'laid back' was just a figure of speech here! My seat was a long bench seat in a small, box-like compartment in this rather old and drab carriage and it was rock hard.

Coming back into reality, I looked around at the rest of the carriage. Perhaps the train should have been named the 'Western Express' as the carriage looked like it had just come from the set of a John Wayne western. It had a series of small, waist-high wooden compartments on either side of a narrow aisle. I had entered from the station's platform, where I had left my father and my quietly weeping mother, via a set of small wooden steps which lead up onto a small stage at the end of the carriage. This separated it from the stage of the next carriage by a small wrought-iron balcony. Looking around the carriage, I felt that at any moment the Wild Bunch, Butch Cassidy or Ned Kelly and his gang of Bushrangers would burst in from the opposite end of the carriage with a loud 'hands up. This is a stick up!'

The windows could be shut by raising them but were usually in the open position because their upper catch would be too worn to hold the window shut. They also had a set of slatted wooden shutters which could be pulled down, but they too did not work. Perhaps in days past and in another country, these shutters would be closed to prevent arrows and spears from reaching John and the good folk herein but now, in 1965 it was probably only to prevent the glare of the sun but not the dust.

There was little of that glare now as we slowly pulled out of one of the many platforms of Sydney's Central Station, designated as Country, and headed southwest towards the Great Dividing Range. This was the low-lying mountain chain which ran down the length of eastern Australia and separated the narrow coastal strip from the great sprawling plains and deserts in the west.

I was now headed more south than west and onto the elevated foothills of this range where a large piece of my home state of New South Wales had been taken out as the Australian Capital Territory. This had reluctantly come about in 1911, ten years after the founding of the Commonwealth of Australia and its separation from its former 'mother country' of Great Britain. The colonial politicians who had spent many years bickering about how to found a new country from six belligerent and uncooperative and separate British colonies, had not been able to decide where the new nation's capital should be. Naturally, Sydney had claimed the right as it was the first city founded in 1788 when the First Fleet brought the sweepings of the goals from Great Britain to these hostile shores. This was absolute nonsense to the good people of Melbourne, the capital of the Colony of Victoria as they had been founded by free settlers, not grubby convicts, and were now the cultural centre of Australia. The other four former colonies were too small or remote to argue against such strong opinions. In a rush to get the new country away from the apron strings of Britannia, the first parliament and the proclamation about the founding of the new country was held in Melbourne – the stench of colonial convicts seemed to be too strong for the sensitive noses of southern politicians. Way to the north, the Colony of Queensland, often referred to as the 'deep north', just couldn't care about the opinions of any southerners but reluctantly agreed anyway - for American readers, one should see Australia's 'deep north' as akin to the 'deep south' in their country. Eventually, after even more bickering between the states of the new Commonwealth, it was decided to 'acquire' land roughly halfway between Sydney and Melbourne and detached it from New South Wales where a new Federal Capital would be built from scratch.

The land chosen was, appropriately for politicians, a former sheep station situated in a long valley running roughly north to south which occasionally suffered earth tremors as it lay between two long fault lines. Running across this valley was a small stream. A competition was started for the new city's design and it was won by the American landscape architect, Walter Burley Griffin. His plan envisaged a series of inter-connected circles which defined the city's centre and outer suburbs. These were connected by many roads set as spokes to these circles. A complex system of road rules greatly dissimilar to those of other states evolved and politicians and other visitors to the capital have been going around in circles ever since.

By 1965, the building of the capital had progressed to a reasonable level with a temporary Parliament House and other large government buildings set around a new, ornamental lake set in its centre. The lake had been named after the city's founding architect and had been formed by damming the small river which had trickled across the valley. Department by department, Federal Government employees and their families had been moved from their secure positions in Sydney, Melbourne and the other state capitals into their new homes in Canberra. The quick development of this hub of government was so rapid that it was often difficult for the inhabitants and the government to keep up. In one week, a whole area of native forest and scrub would be quickly deforested and scraped clean. In the next week a system of circular sealed roads would appear. These usually contained many dead ends and cul-de-sacs which eventually only added more to the confusion of future motorists. Houses and blocks of flats, all of similar design, would then be built as a 'job lot' and introduced European and American ornamental plants would be quickly planted until the entire suburb looked like something out of 'Home and Garden' magazines from these foreign countries. Finally, the immigrant families of public servants would be brought in and housed in their appropriate zones.

"Oh! You're from the Department of Administrative Administration?" some Grand High Poohbah in charge of placements would say to the tired immigrants. "You are to be settled here!" the worthy would sweep his pudgy hand over a map on which the ink was still drying and the family would then head off into the new territory.

Infrastructure such as hospitals, schools, the fire and ambulance services were thought of last of all and the new Australian Capital Territory administration suddenly realised that their public servants were not trained for such lowly careers, so staff for these services had to be imported from New South Wales. Of course, there would be a multimillion-pound [1] building program to house such services and modern equipment would be supplied to suit the showplace setting of the new city. After all, foreign diplomats and other visitors to Australia would need to see that the country was modern, progressive and very wealthy. It was to this rather false environment that I was now trundling slowly but surely in the ancient carriages of the National Capital Express.

The rocking of the carriage and the various sounds of the rolling stock put me into a state of drowsiness as we passed of the green coastal plain and into the dry foothills. My mind went back to my own school days and my drive to become a teacher.

"I am going to be a teacher when I grow up!" a determined little Shipley had announced at age four and I recalled my very first day at school way back in that distant past. Well, fifteen years was a long time for someone who had only just turned nineteen and was now a fully-trained member of the teaching profession. My school life began at the beginning of 1950, the day after my great announcement to my astonished mother. I was probably still too young for school, but I was very keen to

---

[1] Decimal currency and Dollars was yet to be introduced, the old British system still being used.

go as most of my childhood friends had already enrolled and this was something new and exciting. My mother had other ideas as I was her only child and she was reluctant to let me go. As a rule, women did not work in those days and the country was still getting over the massive losses in manpower and material due to the recent Second World War and now there was another war going on in Korea. She had been a country girl, the daughter of the town blacksmith, but the entire family had moved into the city during the Great Depression and it became clear that horses had too much competition from motor vehicles. My father had also gravitated to the city from the family farm and worked on the docks loading cargo and then during the war painting mangled ships at the Navy's dockyard.

Still, my first day at school was full of wonder and I found it difficult to take in all of the sights, sounds and smells of our local Infants School. This was located at a lengthy walk or tram ride from our home in a working-class suburb in southern Sydney. The school was a large complex of connected two-story cream-coloured brick buildings with tall windows and extensive playgrounds of bitumen and a little grass. Such buildings were common around the State and denoted a frenzy of building activity and interest in Education which usually came in sudden bursts of political expediency. Mother and I walked down a long, sunlit corridor with the matronly Headmistress of the Infants Department. The floor boards gleamed white and the light coming through the tall windows to one side gave the corridor an open and friendly appeal. On the other side of the corridor were the classrooms. These were also well-lit by windows which opened onto the corridor and also across each room on the outside of the building. As with most schools today, a long line of bag racks lined the wall of the corridor opposite each classroom.

I shook my hand loose from the tight grip of my mother's hand and ran into the empty classroom close at hand. It was a wonderful room; there were small, coloured felt mats everywhere on the floor and small tables and chairs placed here and there. Cuttings of animals and flowers adorned the walls and some of the windows. A large map hung on the rear wall with the British Empire marked out in brilliant red; the Mother Country was still embedded as part of our country's culture. In the front of the room, extending across most of the width of the room was the blackboard. Actually, it was a dark green colour but all such boards were referred to a 'black'. There were a few pieces of coloured chalk sitting in the runnel below the board and I seized a stick of this wonderful material and started to draw. It confirmed my intensions of the previous day!

I was quickly and unceremoniously extracted and returned to my mother who was taking this separation very hard. The smell of new leather school satchels, including my own highly polished one, and that of sour milk from yesterday's Government daily milk ration to children, only added to the drama of the departure. Soon I was taken and quietly introduced to my new teacher and her class of about forty similarly bewildered children. What a lovely lady! Miss Hirst was her name and she would be the epitome of culture and kindness for the next two years.

Infants School eventually became Primary School and I had established myself as a keen, probably over enthusiastic student who always had his hand up whenever a question was asked or a volunteer needed. I got on fairly well with my fellow classmates but occasionally became the target for any number of school bullies who thought that a skinny, red-haired kid with large teeth was an easy target. These young oafs, destined to become the most belligerent members of our future society and potential politicians, used-car salesmen and criminals, where usually ignored my me and this only made them more unsure of themselves. Besides, I had several older friends at school who were only too happy to help out at such times. School was generally a happy place except for the many times when some of the grumpier teachers targeted me for discipline. Being of a naturally excitable personality, I found that my general enthusiasm for every distraction around me and talking about such events were often not appreciated by the teacher who was attempting to teach the rest of the class. For such disruptions, I was often taken outside and given 'two of the best', one sharp swing downward of the cane on each hand. This hurt for a while but did little to curb my general enthusiasm and gave me some credibility with the more hardened students of the class. It was a good day when I did not get the cane for talking. My enthusiasm continued on well past the lives of these frustrated teachers and many years well past my retirement from their profession.

Near the end of Primary School, whilst I was in Grade Six, all classes in that grade were given an examination. This was a very serious affair and was held in the school assembly hall. Up until then we had sat for smaller tests in our own class in various subjects and I had performed reasonably well but I did not think of my self as a 'brilliant scholar'. No one in my extended family of uncles, aunts and cousins had progressed far within the education system and as was common at that time left school at age fifteen, or earlier if they could get away with it, and get a job.

This examination was, as I later found out, was what was called a 'performance test' and was designed to measure something vague about the student's ability and to allocate students to Secondary School and eventually into channelled employment. Up until now, my education had been a general one of the Three R's as well as Geography, Music and Sport and it was shared within co-educational classes of mixed abilities. The results of this test were then used by the school authorities, generally termed 'Careers Advisor' who would 'recommend' the appropriate secondary School and its courses to suit my newly-found abilities. At the interview with such a worthy, my mother was told that I had a good general ability, especially in mathematics and should enrol in Madgewick Boys High School in the Two-language Commercial course as I would one day make an ideal accountant. This proclamation was taken very well by my mother who did not want her sensitive young son becoming a maintenance worker like most of her many brothers and their children.

I did not understand the significance of this until later when I learnt that most of my friends in my class had been designated as potential Tradesmen and were being sent to Southside Intermediate Technical High School which was situated across the road from my home. Most of the girls from my class were channelled into an equivalent Intermediate High across the road from our primary school to undertake secretarial and domestic science courses so that they could become future office workers and housewives. A small group of my Grade Six colleagues who had showed exceptional ability where to be sent to the city's most prestigious high school which was run by the state but was also part of the Greater Public-School system of wealthy private schools. They would, it was assumed, go on to university, where their parents would pay very high fees for their offspring to become doctors, solicitors, politicians, used-car salesmen and white-collar criminals.

My future school was also considered slightly prestigious and also offered a complete five years of schooling leading to cadetships in some professions and even university if one was lucky. At that time in 1957, only a few students, probably no more than about two percent, went on to do some form of tertiary Education. This would take the form of university for the gifted or wealthy or otherwise Teachers' Colleges, Secretarial and Business Schools and Nursing Colleges. Society was well-ordered and jobs were plentiful. If they did not go on to further education, many students followed in their father's footsteps in trade or commerce and the girls helped their mother at home until they caught some unwary husband – hopefully having had a tertiary education.

Secondary schooling was a lot different in the nineteen sixties than it is today. There have been some good and bad improvements. Today, schools are more open with a liberal education being taught in local high schools with most being coeducational. There seems to be an expectation that all those who are able, and even some who are not, should go on to university with considerable assistance in fees but no idea as to what one will do at the end of the degree, especially getting a job.

Madgwick Boys' High School was a state-run selective high school. This meant that it had five years of schooling in mostly academic subjects and it was assumed that most of its graduates would go onto some form of tertiary education. Forms I to III were highly structured into three strands: academic, commercial and technical with two or three classes of graded ability in each Form. There would be a formal, externally-set examination at the end of Form III called the Intermediate Certificate when most students turned fifteen years of age and were thus old enough to leave school. If one passed that examination, they could then do two more years, graduating at the end of Form V after another externally-set examination called the Leaving Certificate. Students who failed too many yearly examinations in their subjects at any time in their secondary years would be made to repeat that year or leave if they had attained the age of fifteen. It was not too uncommon to have students in Form I who had stayed there for three years until they were able to escape at fifteen or earlier. Students who achieved very good grades at the Leaving Certificate would matriculate and, if they wished to, go on to university or some other tertiary training institution. Those who did not, would get a job or join the Public Service and later become politicians or criminals. Girls who did not fit into any of these occupations stayed at home and helped their mothers until they could trap an unwary male.

Being a potential 'ideal accountant', I was put into the Commercial Stream, second class of Form I and began my studies in Business Principles and Accounting, Mathematics I and II, English, Combined Physics and Chemistry, French and German. Here the wheels began to fall off! No German teacher could be found. It had been a very unpopular career in the 1940's, except in the military, and in 1958 it was no different. So, I did History instead. This and English became my best subjects. Business Principles and Accounting, or BP and A when an economy of words was appropriate, soon showed that becoming an accountant would be as exciting as being sent to Devil's Island, or somewhere similar, to count grains of sand on the beach. Luckily for the next three years we had a great teacher! Mr Smith was his highly uncertain name because he was as Greek-looking as a native of Athens or any of the beautiful islands which I later came to love. Like his (apparent) compatriots he was happy, out-going, friendly and made an incredibly boring subject worth studying. Each lesson he would give us usually consisted of a jumbled set of fictional accounts, sales docents, invoices and small suspicious pieces of paper which had derived from some fictional business of dubious integrity. Well, I assumed that these accounts were fictitious. Perhaps Mr Smith, like many of his colleagues moonlighted elsewhere after school hours. Often, these accounts would be for some seedy hotel with dodgy names such as the Hotel Fred or Hotel Maud which all offered rooms by week, day or, in some cases by the hour. The content of his lessons strongly suggested that Mr Smith had had a varied life before taking up the chalk. His good nature and humour combined with an exceptional ability to tell stores and listen to our questions gave him almost perfect class attentiveness and discipline. We would quietly get on writing up our ledgers – now, was it debit on the left and credit on the right or the reverse? I now know the correct answer to this rhetorical question as I fouled up my first account and had to write out this mantra at home two hundred times!

During this hard leger sorting, Mr Smith would sit back in his chair on the small stage in front of the classroom and muse aloud what he was going to do to his, so-called and probably fictional, unruly lower class called Form IE. Throwing a hand grenade into their room at the end of the lesson, or having them walk across the busy main road outside and hiring a fleet of buses to run them down was just two of the more humane punishments that would be meted out to hapless I E! Having achieved his preferred way with Form IE he could then retire happily at the end of the day to his particular cupboard to be locked in until the start of the next school day. Or so he recounted. We in Form IA (BP & A) thought these statements to be great fun!

I soon discovered that future accountants would also need to be good at mathematics. Calculators and computers had yet to be invented, other than slide rules and table of logarithms, to schools so we needed to have good arithmetical abilities. I did not understand how Pythagoras' Theorem would help me in accounting unless it was to 'balance the books' and algebra was simply an unholy marriage between mathematics and a depleted alphabet. The dubious results of my performance test in Sixth Grade somehow did not match current reality and my marks in Mathematic I and II dropped consistently over the next three years. During this time I blamed my teacher who had me for those three years, but it was more likely my disinterest and lack of work. However, I did not quite like his style of teaching which meant that for most of the lessons he would say something like:

"Shut up! Get out your text books. Open at page so-and-so, copy it out and do all of the exercises."

He would then lean back on his chair and pick his nose and rub his hands over his balding head. Perhaps he had discovered some secret to hair restoration. Any noise from the class was punished by being sent out of the classroom or more likely some sarcastic remark, usually to me or one of my friends. In addition, we all had to suffer his stories of his survival as a young man in the Great Depression.

Talking about survival, at the end of Form III, I had miraculously survived the Intermediate Certificate with reasonably good grades including an unbelievable Pass in mathematics. This joy was short-lived as I graduated into Form IV's notorious General Mathematics class the next year. This seemed to be the dumping ground for all of the students who had low scores in maths and for many, all the other subjects as well. We were given yet another old teacher whom we hoped would suddenly succumb to old age before he got to his daily lesson plan of telling us which page numbers we had to copy out and the exercise to do. It was a wonder that anyone learnt anything in that over-crowded mathematics class. In that class there also were a good proportion of students who had passed their schooling 'use by date' at fifteen years of age but who were there only because their parents and the system had nowhere else for them to go. At the end of the year things were pretty sad; discipline had degenerated to a succession of canings and failures at tests and our futures looked dim.

Then, after a few weeks of this torture, the school suddenly changed our subject to a new course called 'Mathematics III' which was a highly condensed version of the better and more practical parts of the two other mainstream maths courses. The new textbook for this course was both legible and contained some English statements of simple explanation in addition to the usual jumble of Greek alphabet and meaningless symbols and numbers. Moreover, unlike our old General Maths course, this new mathematics was considered to be of matriculation standard. Hooray! It was still taught by the same doddering old teacher who unfortunately had not yet succumbed to old age, and still used the same teaching method of having us open the textbook each lesson, copying pages and doing the exercises but at last these pages contained readable English as well as the undecipherable hieroglyphs of Greek letters, numbers and symbols. The exercises were now at least more interesting and even algebra and calculus become almost understandable. At the externally-set Leaving Certificate examination I received yet another great surprise by gaining a healthy 'B' grade pass.

Now at the end of my junior year in Form III and to the great horror of the school authorities and possibly also to my mother, I dropped BP and A along with the untidy mish-mash of Combined Physics and Chemistry and took a more science-oriented course with separate Physics and Chemistry in Form IV. There goes another future deficiency in the ledger of names in the accountancy profession!

Whilst English and History were my best subjects, and I was in the top 'A' class for these subjects, science had become my hobby at home as well as one of my preferred school subjects. History in particular was extremely interesting to me and still is today. Our teacher, Mr. Dominic was urbane and an excellent teacher who made the subject live. We all called him the 'Jesuit' behind his back with all due respect, as someone had said that he had once been a Catholic priest. School students are good at spreading rumours, as teenagers often take up one small snippet of information and expanded it greatly by applying their natural sense of vivid imagination. This is probably a natural biological process enabling them to explore their surroundings as they got older but is lost in adulthood unless they become teachers of authors. Unfortunately, this also sometimes becomes a source of frustration and rebellion when they find out later in life that their imagination and reality are two different constructs.

We did a lot of Russian history, which was very exciting and my small group of friends in the class, aptly named the 'Komsomol' after the Soviet's youth league, would help Mr. Dominic, again behind his back, by purchasing copies of 'Soviet Union' magazine from the friendly Communist street-seller and then placing it in his desk drawer before class. He would smile and thank his unknown benefactors for this most recent view of the political reality of the world and get on with his lesson. As a reminder of Mr Dominic's excellent teaching, members of the Komsomol later climbed up onto the roof of his teaching block and cemented a large home-made Soviet flag into the guttering during the last week of Form V. It was still flying many months after we had left the school!

Our English teacher was another person whom we all admired. Mrs O'Grady was a middle-age lady dressed in very sober clothing and had a delightful Irish accent. She put considerable charm and realism in her readings of the set novels which we had to study. She did not find it difficult to quieten any slightly-disruptive student as she did it with a friendly smile and some delightful lilting phrase like:

"Now, then to be sure, yuh railly dahn't want to do dat, now wooehldn't you?"

We had to study the novel 'Silas Marner - the Weaver of Raveloe' by George Elliot and we found it hard going. To overcome this irksome task, yet another rumour was circulated that she not only made her own conservative dresses but probably wove the cloth as well on her own loom at home. Another rumour spread to the younger students of any new incoming Form I was that she was really a Cailleach[2] and would turn naughty boys into leprechauns. Mrs O'Grady was a wonderful teacher and her English with an Irish lilt was a delight to learn from.

My grades in the junior years had put me into the 'C' class for both Physics and Chemistry, but that was acceptable to me as I was only generally acceptable as a student to the teacher as well. Physics went along with the usual experiments which sometimes did not work or at others produced a lot of meaningless data which was difficult to translate into reality. Again, we were blessed with a good teacher, Mr Stubbins who was a younger man and rather

---

[2] A Cailleach (pronounced "kyle-yeukh") is a Celtic witch.

thick set. Because of this we called him 'The Chest' and generally got on well with him and so there were few of our 'tricks' in his class. His physics lessons, however did introduce me to the use of high voltage and how an old car's induction coil could produce some interesting effects if wired to the metal doorknob of the classroom.

Chemistry and I had a natural affinity as I had a long history of dabbling with various concoctions at home; mostly in the explosive category. I had been given a small book called 'Chemistry Experiments for Boys and Girls', another item so rare nowadays but would probably be banned as a potential terrorist's handbook. It contained not only many wonderous and exciting experiments but also how to get chemicals from common places such as grocery and hardware stores or how to make then from other household substances. My favourite recipe was that for making nitrocellulose, or the highly explosive 'gun cotton' used in naval artillery, out of cotton wool or ping pong balls. Luckily, my procedure was unproductive as well as inexplosive, so I turned to making 'flash powder' from household ammonia and tincture of iodine from the medicine cabinet. This book continued on with me well into my career after leaving school and into my own professional career.

Our teacher Mr Dudley was a total loss when it came to teaching and chemistry for that matter! We just called him 'Dud' and tried as often as we could to set him up in class, mostly during the once-a-fortnight laboratory class. On one occasion, with some chemical solution bubbling away in a beaker set on a gauze and tripod over a Bunsen burner, we added a drop of red ink from someone's fountain pen. This spread out in the solution and gave it a cheerful pink colour:

"Sir! Sir!" I cried "Look what's happened to our solution!"

Dud immediately rushed to our desk, peered this way and that to see what was going on and then proceeded to write down various chemical equations on my book to see why there should have been a colour change. No luck.

"Must be a change in its pH[3]." He ventured much to our hidden joy and left it at that. He didn't have a clue at the best of times.

My co-conspirators in the chemistry class also had an activity against some of the class 'crawlers' who always did have an answer to Dud's own weird chemistry

[3] pH is a measure of the acidity of a substance and it ranges from strong acid of 1 to strong alkali at 14. Universal Indicator goes through a range of colours with different levels of pH.

questions. This was to quickly steal their metal ruler and heat the end over the Bunsen flame. We would then replace the ruler just as quickly so that its end was hanging over the desk. With some luck, on our part not the victim's, he would pick up the rule at the hot end with an appropriate yell of unexpected pain and yet another problem for Dud to solve.

In my first year in the Senior year, my good friend Peter Ross, usually shortened to 'Petros', and I managed somehow to be selected as Laboratory Prefects. Professional adult Laboratory Managers had not yet been introduced to schools, and the over-worked Head of Science was expected to purchase, prepare solutions, do all of the safety audits and everything else required to manage six laboratories in a school of about 1200 potentially-dangerous teenagers. Petros and I had to perform all of the lowly tasks such as sweeping and cleaning up the preparation room, washing all of the glassware, scrubbing all of the laboratory benches and stocking the reagent bottles with fresh solutions.

This job also meant also that we had the advantage of stocking our own chemistry sets at home but we also learnt much more practical science than our classmates. I might add here, that those were the 'good old days' of the home chemistry set when young children could go into most pharmacies or chemical supply companies in the city and purchase almost anything:

"Nitro-glycerine? Yeah kid. How many bottles would you like?" would be the seller's response to our harmless request.

Well, perhaps it wasn't that easy to get explosives, but most of the usual school chemicals and equipment could be easily purchased over the counter. Many children at that time had chemistry sets as there was not any television, computers or other electronic games. Fireworks were another commodity which junior pyromaniacs could also purchase in bulk and a few weeks before 'cracker night' as the Empire or Guy Fawkes celebration was held, local toy shops would sell a great variety of seemingly harmless explosive devices. These were useful in blowing up letter boxes of any unpleasant neighbour.

There were other ancient and honourable activities at home such as tree-house building and billy-cart construction at which I was also an expert. I had built a shack in the corner of our fenced yard in which I practiced my mystic art of schoolboy chemistry. My father was a great guy and every inch a 'John Wayne' character in build and temperament. He was tolerant enough to let my friend Petros and I get on with our experiments despite the occasional fire and disgusting odours which sometimes occurred. At school, we had soon ceased to be targets of any school bully who previously thought of us as nerds and therefore easy prey. Any threat by some tough character was soon dealt with using some 'weapon of mass destruction – individual variety'.

The most potent treatment involved the use of calcium carbide, a chemical used in old miners' carbide lamps and which could be purchased in large tins from any hardware store which sold lamps. This solid would react with water to produce very smelly, impure and explosive acetylene gas. Now our desks in class also had holes or ink wells into which small containers of ink were once placed even before our time but which were now not used due to the arrival of ink-filled fountain pens. At the start of the class, a fellow conspirator would get in first and place a small plastic open pill bottle containing a little water under the ink well opening of our target's desk. We had arranged seating in each class so our target's desk was easy to locate. As the rest of the class entered, I would quickly drop a gelatine capsule full of calcium carbide into the ink well hole and therefore into the water in the container below. The victim, usually one of the class bullies would take his seat and the rest class would quietly sit up straight for the arrival of the teacher. Now the gelatine capsule, purchased by the large box from the friendly pharmacy, would take about a minute to dissolve and then the carbide would react with the water. This would soon produce an unbelievably bad odour coming from the bully's area. There would be the usual finger-pointing at the smelly offender with loud communal cries of:

"Sir! Bloggs just broke wind! Get him out!"

Bully Bloggs would soon be hustled out of the room and given a stern lecture on his poor digestive habits by the teacher. Unfortunately, on some occasions, the gas became too much and we would all have to evacuate the room; all of us giving Bloggs a hard time as we went out.

Our carbide capsules also worked well in the Boys' Toilet, habituated at lunchtime by a group of aggressive and territorial smokers who persisted in throwing their butts into a flushing toilet when finished. Sick of this anti-social behaviour, we substituted our own by sticking a lump of solid carbide up under the rim of the toilet using chewing gum. Flushing the toilet gave a good amount of acetylene which ignited in a bright flash when a lighted cigarette butt was thrown in. These and other 'devices' added to the fun of attending school and set the scene for a lifetime of teaching 'interesting chemistry' to new generations of students who also seemed to love the unexpected.

My secondary education finished with a good matriculation at the end of 1962, although at the time, our future seemed to be uncertain. America and the USSR were at loggerheads and Kennedy had threatened Khrushchev with nuclear retaliation if he sent any more missiles to Cuba, so in our little world there was a lot of uncertainty. Thankfully, this 'missile crisis' blew over and we were faced with the task of getting a job or doing more study. By this time, my desire to become a teacher was just as strong as it was in 1950 so I applied for a Teachers' Scholarship. Anyone going on to tertiary studies then had to have either won a fee-paying scholarship, cadetship with some company, won a government scholarship or have parents who could afford a very large amount of money for tuition fees and living expenses. Luckily there were many scholarships and cadetships available and so at the end of Form V I had applied for a wide range of these benefits and had also done the entrance exams for both the State and Federal Public Services. These I passed and also was offered cadetships in the Commonwealth Bank (oh no! more accountancy!), as a Surveyor and then a university scholarship as a Forester in the Commonwealth's Forestry Service. Just before accepting the latter, I received notification of acceptance as a trainee primary school teacher to the Teachers' College. All other offers were then gratefully declined.

Chapter Two: Lumen Siccum

I was suddenly jerked into consciousness as the carriage did a double take and jostled into the one in front. The train had come to a halt at a small siding to allow a bigger and more important freight train to pass. It did so with an arrogant flash of multicoloured walls, a loud rush of air and clatter of many wheels on rails.

I looked out of my window which had again dropped down to emit a suffocating mixture of hot dust and diesel fumes. We had stopped somewhere in the middle of nowhere. The greenery of the coastal plain had given way now to the endless brown, drab plains of the Southern Tablelands. The country seemed endless and had been cleared many years for sheep grazing and erosion. There were a few pitiful clumps of stunted gum trees hugging together to keep out the dust and the ubiquitous lines of barbed-wire fencing going hither and thither over the low rounded light brown hills. The grass everywhere was also stunted and brown having struggled and lost, giving up its valuable moisture to the hot, dry air. I watched this sad panorama for a while and then the train went across a small road bridge and the highway suddenly appeared close to the tracks. The Hume Highway was not terribly grandiose in those days; simply one lane each side of a faint, semi-erased dotted central line; the only sign of some prestige denoting it as a major highway. There were few cars on it going in both directions and occasionally a long semi-trailer carrying its forlorn cargo of bleating sheep destined for the tables of the city. Telegraph poles flashed past at fairly regular intervals, some on the hillside slopes slightly tilted over where the soil had moved on its relentless journey downhill. Beautiful in its emptiness but tiring after watching it for a while, the swaying motion and the jingle jangle of the carriage once again caused my head to droop and my mind to go back to past dreams.

I was now in my best suit and with a short back-and-sides haircut. I had taken the bus from home into the city and then walked to the hallowed gatehouse of the University. Perhaps it was due to some perverse principle of economy or a desire to keep all unruly students together which led the education authorities to build the Teachers College within the University grounds. After all, it was an independent institution, although the University did reluctantly give up some of its graduates to attend their post-graduate year in the College's Diploma of Education one-year program. The two-year courses offered at the Teachers' College, mainly for Infants and Primary teachers, could hardly be compared to this august diploma as its students also possessed that piece of paper from the University showing their superiority in having obtained a degree. Possibly the University was grateful for passing its graduates onto the College. Afterall it wasn't a real post-graduate course which would lead to even higher university degrees such as a Masters or Doctorate. Not having a university degree was no problem on my part, as I did not think that I was university material anyway and I had already achieved a far greater opportunity in gaining a place to train as a teacher.

Wandering into the University in my brand-new grey suit and clutching my brand-new simulated leather briefcase, I felt that perhaps I should also have painted a large yellow target on my back. There were many other students walking in my direction early this morning as lectures for some would start soon at nine. I felt rather over-dressed and uneasy as the standard dress for university students in 1963 did not include a suit, tie and briefcase. Nor a clean shirt, tie, polished shoes and short hair for that matter. College students stood out in the crowd of torn jeans, anti-everything T-shirts, long hair and sandals – if it was a formal day. The Teachers' College maintained a set of very strict codes of dress and behaviour. Afterall, we were to become teachers! - still regarded as one of the main pillars of society at that time. Men, and even naïve and callow youths of 17, were instructed to wear clean suits, or with some reluctant allowance, slacks and sports coat, and especially a clean shirt with an appropriate coloured tie. Hair was to be cut short and the large number of textbooks we had to carry would be done so in an appropriate briefcase. Young ladies were to be neatly attired in a dress, which ended below the knee, and the colour of which, should certainly not be red. Nor should they show bare shoulders as this was thought to inflame the passions of the surrounding males. Thick stockings had to be worn by all ladies, even in the hot summers and these, my colleagues complained, were like wearing plastic bags on their legs. Boy! were we targets for the 'great unwashed' at the University!

Life has a way of favouring the innocent. On my first day at the College, sitting in its Great Hall amongst other clones in suits or non-red dresses with covered shoulders, the guest speaker was ninety-year old Jack Lang, a former Premier of the state and a well-known firebrand in politics. Considered one of Australia's great and volatile politicians, he had shown no sign of slowing down at ninety and gave us a rousing speech akin to that of any evangelist exhorting us to go forth and take the 'dry light' of learning to the masses of New South Wales. The College's motto was 'Lumen Siccum' or 'dry light' and this had been taken from one of the sayings of the Ancient Greek, Heraclitus the Obscure:

"Lumen siccum optima anima" loosely translated as "The most perfect mind is a dry light."

Later upon reflection and having discovered the meaning of this mystic motto, I wondered at the immense task that the College faced with its new cohort of students whose minds seem to be less than perfect, especially my fellow students who were even now wondering what red dresses and bare shoulders would look like on the greatly larger number of female colleagues who also sat in the hall.

But what an introduction! The Dean of the College then dropped another dramatic bombshell which was to change my life forever. He was embarrassed to admit that the scholarships for the new program in Junior Secondary Science which was to be soon introduced into schools had not been taken up by many students. These were still available should any students now sitting in the hall wished to change their scholarship. The speed of light was slow compared to that of my hand shooting up. What an opportunity! This new scheme was to redress the woeful lack of science teachers in the state by changing the junior secondary courses in schools to four years instead of three and offering a combined junior science program of biology, chemistry, physics and the new school subject of geology. This was my ideal of an excellent life and I felt some sort of divine guidance present in this crowded hall. Now schools were to be more open and not organised along the constraints of future occupations, gender or ability. High schools now would take in local students and provide a broad education in maths, the new science, social science and the arts to all students. The idea of studying geology really was the icing on the cake.

Over a year ago, whilst I was still in Grade V, I had been inspired by the Disney movie 'Journey to the Center of the Earth'. This was a good version of Jules Verne's novel which I had read until the pages fell off. Having seen Disney's version of what was below the Earth and the portrayal of the fictional character of his Professor Lindenbrook of the Geology Faculty of Edinburgh University, I had joined a local caving club. Grossly under age, I had started my own journeys below the Earth with the totally unconventional members of the club. Soon, whilst still at school, I had become a Trip Leader of the club and led my own expeditions to explore and map limestone caves in the mountains to Sydney's west. Studying geology, now formally, was of great excitement to me and it would in the future open up an entirely new pathway for me.

Back above ground in the Great Hall, the new acolytes who had volunteered for this new course were given an appropriate room number and we stood up and slowly eased our way out of the aisles past the assembled multitude who gave us all looks varying from bemusement to pity.

It eventuated that this program attracted more than its share of eccentrics. My new classmates were a mixture of young and old, but mainly young, former school leavers. The older set, we later found out, were those who had failed in their attempts to obtain a university degree and so decided to go into teaching or those who had come from another career and decided also to join the profession. I have always objected to the foolish statement that 'those who can't do, go into teaching' because it was usually said by someone who could neither do nor teach. The younger group of which I was one, mostly included those who had left school and genuinely wished to follow a teaching career. A few, like their counterparts in their first year at university, really did not have a clue about what career they should take and teaching looked like a good idea at the time. Their scholarship paid for their tuition and also gave a small 'living allowance' and a textbook grant. Luckily, I still lived at home because the so-called 'living allowance 'of nine pounds, sixteen shillings[4] a fortnight would hardly pay for rent, let alone

---

[4] Prior to 1966, decimal currency had yet to be introduced and the old British system of twelve pennies to one shilling and twenty shillings to a pound was still in use. In 1966, one pound became $2.

food and transport. The basic wage at that time was fourteen pounds, fifteen shillings and six pence per week.

By-and-large, the Junior Secondary Teaching class were a good group dominated by the younger set who were generally tolerated in good friendship by our older and more mature colleagues. The program was going to be an intense and rather concentrated program of learning in a great variety of subjects. As this was a new course designed to spearhead the new science program in secondary schools, the general philosophy was one of scholarship and evangelism.

We even had our own 'Bible': a very thick book which was to be the new textbook for the unsuspecting high school students of the future. It was about the same size and thickness of a desktop King James version of the real thing and was extremely heavy. It had been produced by a consortium of science academics from the University who were listed, with their photographs and many degrees, on the inside front pages. It was going to be a daunting task to get through such a great amount of material in two years, not to mention the damage it was going to do to my thin briefcase and arm muscles. It also came with a 'Teachers' Edition' which was almost as thick as the original. This was a very useful book as it contained all of the answers to the many student questions in the textbook and hints as to how to teach each chapter and other useful information. This included suggested experiments, methods of obtaining equipment, how to look after laboratory livestock (what?), preparation of chemical solutions and all of those other skills and recipes that would be needed by the neophyte in schools which as yet had no professional laboratory managers. We had also been given a recommendation to buy the 'UNESCO Source Book for Science Teaching', another condensed guide for those unfortunates who went out into the more remote parts of the world to teach science with whatever homemade equipment they could make, beg, borrow or steal. We all wondered just what we had let ourselves into and what really was the condition of some of the schools in our state.

There was another major difference between the Teachers' College and the university which contained it. Our program was to be a formal one and not unlike an older version of a very academic high school. Lectures ran from nine in the morning to usually about four or five in the afternoon for five days a week and were compulsory with a roll being taken at the start of each lecture. This timetable varied slightly on Friday mornings which were set aside as 'Observation' time for visiting local schools to see how selected professionals did the job of inculcating shallow minds with the higher notions of science. When there were no observations to be made, we were allowed to arrive after our usual lunch hour on Fridays. We were exhorted to spend these free mornings in practicing writing on the blackboards in the College basement or at other intellectual pursuits. My friends and I usually went to the local bar which seemed to have no knowledge of the new eighteen-years-of-age restrictions. Our lecture immediately after our liquid lunch on Friday was Health. This was given by an old, retired former GP who had found it easier to work at the College than to be in practice. Whatever his reasons for being there, his course of instruction and the manner in which it was delivered was somewhat like a continual mundane sermon on the evils of drinking and smoking. This often went completely over the heads of the class, especially of the Drinking Set who had just returned from the local bar and whose members had also taken up smoking many years before.

Not all lectures were like those of Health. We had a very broad and, in some subjects, an in-depth education as well. Mostly our lecturers were former high school teachers who knew their subject and how to teach it very well and had been successful enough to acquire their prestigious position at the Teachers' College. Indeed, our lecturer in English Literature was Mrs. O'Grady, one of my former teachers at Madgwick and she was delighted see me again as I had been one of her best students. It would be good to hear her delightful Irish account of some of the world's best literature and I hoped that Silas Marner would not be included.

Apart from Health and English Literature, we had lectures in Biology, Chemistry, Geology, Physics, Mathematics, Child Psychology, Education, Speech, Government and Politics, Sport and Teaching Method. This latter program was somewhat disappointing as the lecturer hardly ever showed up and when he did, he delivered his information in a sleepy monotone. Moreover, his own teaching method was somewhat akin to that of my former mathematics teachers at Madgwick in which most of the lecture involved group discussions on obscure topics such as how to design the cover of a student's formal practical book. He once had a good name in the state's teaching profession but had 'retired' to the College after 'burning out' in front of the classroom where he had remained well after his retirement age.

There was also an elective subject which we could take to improve our general intellect other than being 'rude mechanicals' as Shakespeare had said in 'A Midsummer's Night Dream'. Our choice was to be either drama, music or art. I liked drawing, especially at Madgwick on my former teachers' blackboards before class, and so I took the art elective. This was a good choice as our lecturer was a former well-known artist of previous years who had taken this job between exhibitions. Hank, as he insisted, we call him, was about sixty years of age and full of vigour. He had spent much of his time in the art scene of London and New York and several of his modernist paintings hung in our city's Art Gallery.

Lectures were greatly varied and we often did not know what to expect. There were no notes to be taken as this was meant to be a leisure elective (his words!). On some days he would issue large sheets of paper and charcoal and select the most useless individual from the class of which there were a few as we were a mixed group from all of the College's programs. This unfortunate being would then act as our model and would be sat upon a chair set up on top of a table. As befitted the importance of this program, lectures were held in a classroom of an old condemned school which sat just outside of the University grounds and was referred to as 'The Annex'. Our task then would be to draw this personage using the technique of the day. This style may involve the use of curves only, straight lines and angles (his favourite and personal style) only or simply free sketching. The resulting 'art work' was, to say, incredibly unattractive, although I have seen worse hanging in galleries. At other times, Hank would tell us tales about his time in New York when he and his friends spent more time debunking local art critics than producing real art. Perhaps one of the best stories involved a pet chimpanzee which one of his set had borrowed from a local socialite. They had spread a large piece of canvas on the floor of their little apartment and had given the chimp copious supplies of paint. The delighted animal literally 'went ape' and produced a ghastly, multicoloured mess. The best part of this 'art work' was cut out, framed and signed by one of the better-known buddies and sent to a local gallery for display. When it received rave reviews from one of their favourite critics, Hank and his buddies then confessed their act to the media which then commented on the questionable artistic ability of the hapless critic. Near the end of the year, Hank left. No doubt he had a new exhibition forthcoming and better career prospects.

Our new lecturer in Elective Art was a vastly different kettle of fish – not a completely inaccurate metaphor. She was not interested in any hands-on work but was more interested in teaching Art History and Appreciation as an academic subject. Every lecture was one of copious note-taking with the occasional showing of a sample art work. After Hank's humane approach, these notes were hard work. At least I got to appreciate the French Impressionists and saw that there was considerable

Monet[5] to be made in art. To add insult to our injury, she announced that there would be a formal examination at the end of the year which would be counted towards our yearly assessment. We expected a written exam with detailed questions on art history such as:

'In no more than five pages suggest why during the 1870 war in France that Lautrec had nothing Toulouse?[6]"

Instead, she produced easels and large volumes of Hank's art paper and paints and gave us all one hour in which to produce a painting in water colour. This was a major setback. Some of my colleagues could only draw in curves and others using lines and angles! I was determined that she was not to get me down so I set to with large amounts of red, yellow, orange and brown paint on my 'canvas'. I was still actively engaged in caving outside of College so I drew a typical caver in muddy brown overalls, helmet and lamp treading his way through a maze of pointed stalactites and stalagmites coming from the ceiling and ground respectively. In the end I was very happy with my work. Hank would have been proud as it came close to Picasso's style even if was unintentional. This must have

---

[5] Oscar-Claude Monet (1840 – 1926) was a French painter and a founder of the French Impressionist style.
[6] Henri de Toulouse-Lautrec (1864 – 1901) among one of the best-known French painters of the Post-Impressionist period.

been also in the mind of our lecturer who decided to grade all of the paintings then and there.

"What a marvellous depiction of a bush-fire fighter and his dangerous environment. It shows an intense appreciation with the emotional aspect of the subject!" she said of my work and promptly gave me a 'Distinction' grade. Who was I to argue? so I accepted this grade graciously.

Biology and Geology were of great interest to me as I had not studied these at high school. Until this new program, boys generally studied physics and chemistry, individually or combined and girls studied biology. Now all science classes in high school were to study all of these sciences in their junior years. How some of the older teachers who had been teaching their very specific brand of science in classes for years would now cope was a matter for some contemplation. But not by an unworldly Education Department which assumed that all teachers were adaptable and could teach any subject.

Education, one of our major subjects and one which should contribute most to our future skills as teachers, was also another joy because of my interest in the subject matter and the personal teaching style of our urbane lecturer. Mr. Wells was probably the most sophisticated member of the College staff. Well-dressed in a stylish suit at all times and with a smooth way of talking. In another life he would have made an ideal politician or used-car salesman. None of his style was at all pretentious or of a socially superior manner, for he was easy to talk to and had an open, friendly method of teaching.

My first encounter with Mr. Wells had been during one of my Practice Teaching sessions out in one of my local schools. He had arrived to assess my ability as a student teacher in the classroom. Whilst the school had a bad reputation, I had got on well with the students because I also came from a similar background and had been able to survive in class and so his inspection periods went quite well for me. The students knew the score and were on my side. Unfortunately, at our post-lesson discussion, I had wandered off the track when he asked me to discuss my overall educational philosophy. At seventeen, such concepts were yet to be developed so I had given him my pseudo-intellectual views that everything was predestined, including my future pathway in education. This normally would have been dismissed as puerile ravings had I not arrived late for my first Education lecture a few months later when I started my second year. It was the first lecture of the day on the first day of College and I had missed my bus. Arriving late and after the rest of the class had been seated, I burst into the room gasping for breath after running the length of the road into the University and then up two flights of stairs. I was greeted with looks of derision from my classmates but a cheerful response from Mr. Wells:

"Ah, Mr, Shipley. Welcome." He said, turning to the class who now had looks of wolfish expectation on their faces.

"At our last meeting, Mr. Shipley had been explaining to me his views on predestination and its ramifications on the intellectual training of adolescents in high schools. Wasn't that so, Mr. Shipley?" he continued.

"Yes, Mr. Wells." I meekly replied and slunk into a seat in the front row.

This introduction to second year Education was nevertheless delivered in Mr. Well's most urbane manner with no trace of sarcasm at all. I had been late to class and this had been the result. I was never late again.

It was in Mr. Well's lectures that I began to understand what the term 'educational philosophy' meant. In an easy manner he explained some of the major theories of education then being used in schools and debated in education circles. I was most impressed with the cognitive ideas of the Swiss psychologist Jean Piaget and the

American Jerome Bruner who suggested that children develop cognitive pathways of understanding by their physical response to experiences such as reading, writing and other practical experiences. Hand-eye coordination was an important mental and physical activity and I began to understand why my many punishments at high school involving the writing out of hundreds of lines made me remember the words which I had written: 'debit is on the left and credit is on the right' from BP and A. Thanks Mr. Smith from Greece! Other concepts fed to our receptive collective consciousness included such ideas as: Constructivism whereby students develop their own insights through experience; Humanism which asserts that learning is a natural process which helps young students to reach self-actualization; and Classical whereby a stimulus can be used to produce a behavioural response. The latter was interesting, especially when we went into the experiments of the Russian Ivan Pavlov. Rather than having dogs salivating when a bell was rung in anticipation for food, we became conditioned when the hands of the classroom clock approached the time for the end of any of our boring lectures such as Health and would upset the old doctor with our salivation.

Mr. Wells also exposed us to the cultural teaching of the Australian satirist Barry Humphreys. As a break from some of the most boring educational theories, Mr. Wells would play a Barry Humphrey vinyl record on a portable record player which he would bring in for such an occasion. Pavlov would have been proud of this form of conditioning as the first sight of the record player in Mr. Well's hand would produce the corresponding salivation and looks of joy in the faces of our class. Classic characters such as Edna Everage, Sandy Stone, that crude epitome of culture Sir Les Patterson and some of the others of Barry Humphrey's invention would leave us with a sense that teaching should be a fun experience as well as how not to behave in society.

In my second year, there wasn't much spare time at College, except on the occasional Friday mornings when we would conveniently forget about delving down into the College basement and practising our blackboard skills which were yet to be learnt. In our lunch hour the Drinking Set would rush out of the University grounds to the local pub and quickly down a few drinks. This was too much excitement for me and I really could not afford it, and besides I had found in first year that I got fairly drunk on only two beers. Instead, a few of my regular friends and I would wander over to the University's Medical School's cafeteria nearby and buy sandwiches or pies; although we did have some suspicions as to what was in Medical School pies!

Being now at the mature age of eighteen, my little group and I had taken to becoming more eccentric than usual. Incensed at having to wear a tie in a place surrounded by university students who were yet to known the meaning of such an item of apparel, I had taken to wearing a cravat instead. The College authorities had reluctantly accepted this as it was in the fine print written at the College's foundation in 1896 that 'gentlemen must wear appropriate neck wear'. My friends thought that this was much too pretentious and some of the others in the College had expressed some doubts about my manliness and cultural sensitivity. To add to this picture of urbanity, I took up smoking a pipe. Smoking cigarettes was almost a mandatory part of adult culture at that time, but I had not taken to the habit. Smoking a pipe, my naïve brain reasoned, would give me some form of adult acceptance, even if I looked like a young, redheaded and skinny teenager. Which I was. Then at the start of my second year, I had a major blow to my cultured self-esteem. The incoming males of the new first year class thought that my dress and smoking habits were the epitome of the potentially socially-conscious teacher. Subsequently they all took to wearing cravats and smoking pipes. Faced with a cohort of clones wearing cravats of many colours and pipes ranging from the long, white meerschaums to the hideous bulbous German variety, I swallowed my pride and reverted to the more mundane sports coat and tie expectation. I still occasionally smoked my pipe but not within the College grounds.

Another dress eccentricity which my small group of friends engaged in was the wearing of our white laboratory coats on all occasions. Almost on a daily basis, the College authorities would be telling us that we were to act like professions and bring the light of science to our darkened world. We had to wear our white coats to all science practical lessons in all four of the sciences which we studied. This meant that at other times we would have to carry them and our heavy briefcase to other lectures and outside the College as well. We had found that the term 'briefcase' was indeed an oxymoron. There was nothing 'brief' about these heavy and over-stuffed cases! Instead of dragging these coats around over our arms we decided to wear them at all times. Some of our non-science lecturers tolerated this apparel and others would tell us to disrobe.

"You look like a bunch of flunkies in a morgue!" was but one of the friendly comments received by these members of staff.

Others were even less complementary. However, we continued to wear our laboratory coats around the College and especially into the small College cafeteria where the

Infants/Primary set would regard us with great suspicion and were not sure as to what to do about these white-coated eccentrics. It all came to a head one day following a three-hour organic chemistry practical session. We had been doing some experiment which involved the use of rather smelly oils and other organic solvents. By about the second hour we had all lost any sense of smell and our coats had taken a careless drenching with these liquids. After the practical session we had innocently wandered into the cafeteria. To the assembled multitude it was as though an entire oil refinery had suddenly come online. With loud hoots and hollers of derision we were pelted with a variety of foods and cardboard cups and plates and told in uncertain terms, which defy public print, never to return.

So, my friends and I of the White Coat set had been banished from the College cafeteria for life. Well, we would go to where white coats were appreciated: the nearby Medical School cafeteria just down the road. Here was a relatively quiet place where many of the medical students congregated for their lunch breaks. Most of them were older than us, were less noisy and more studious; the others from the Medical School who did not come here rubbed shoulders with our own Drinking Set in the local pub. We would buy our drinks and sandwiches, and sometimes a meat pie after a full autopsy of its contents, and sit outside on the lawns in front of the Medical School. Passing university students in their uniforms of torn jeans, anti-everything T-shirts and long, scruffy hair gave us little attention and left us alone for a change. They had given up on the Medical Students who always seemed to be wearing their white coats and were generally considered superior beings who would one day graduate. Occasionally when things were too quiet in the cafeteria, and especially when there were some of the female medical students present, we would start up a simulated conversation something like:

"I say, Dr. Bloggs, what operation did you perform today?" to which a reply might have been:

"Well, Old Chap. I performed a remarkable walletdectomy this morning. The patient didn't feel a thing."

We naturally soon wore out our welcome here as well, so we spent most of second year sitting outside of the College eating our sandwiches which we had been forced to bring from home.

Finally, all good things had to come to an end. Second year College had been hard work but like first year, a lot of fun. My class had been full of good types and many of them had become my good friends and we had had our share of home parties and the occasional social event at the College. We had been able to wander the hallowed grounds of the University and despite our social activities in the Medical School and elsewhere, had been very well-trained in most aspects of becoming a science teacher.

However, the College had one last humiliation to remind us that we were still only to be Probationary Teachers and our Teachers' Certificate would not be issued until after working as classroom teachers for the next two years. This humiliation took the form of a full medical examination to be given by our old doddery friend who had lectured us in Health about the evils of drinking, smoking and generally having a good time. It was embarrassing to stand semi-naked in a draughty hallway in the male section of the small College 'medical centre'. There had always been segregation of the genders wherever possible at the College other than at lectures and public assemblies – no doubt to prevent the males from being over excited at the few rebellious women who wore red dresses with bare shoulders and no stockings. The Education Department, who would be our employer, obviously did not want their expensively-trained products to fail in health or drop dead before setting foot in the classroom. Accordingly, we all had to pass the College medical examination. The 'medical centre' had two small rooms accessed by two long and draughty corridors. In the male corridor I now stood with my fellow near-graduates waiting to be individually ushered into the presence of our medical geriatric for the examination. The girls were to have there turn tomorrow and a real GP of the feminine variety had been hired for this occasion. In turn we were generally given a cursory 'once over' to ensure that we would survive the next two years as Probationary Teachers and not die or develop some medical problem which the Education Department clerks would have to deal with. My height and weight were taken with the sarcastic remark of:

"What do you do in a strong wind, lad?" referring to my generally thin physique.

I doubt that anyone failed this medical exam, as teachers were in short supply and two years of hard work in front of a classroom would probably toughen the spirit if not weaken the body. It was a risk the Department of Education was prepared to take!

The same approach also seemed to be applied to our final examinations which covered a large array of subjects. I had done poorly in Education as I had not learnt off all of the scripts of the Barry Humphries records and so would have to return to the College early next year, my first year as a Probationary Teacher, to re-sit the examination. A couple of my classmates who had drifted into the course without any ideas about becoming science teacher, and certainly not Probationary ones, had several outright failures. Whilst the College authorities made big noises about these massive deficiencies, they condescended to agree to allow these unfortunates to also enter the teaching profession. God help it! Fortune also seemed to favour the not-so-innocent and both of these failures decided that other fields were greener and took a year's leave. They then proceeded to travel overseas to 'Mother England' where they would no doubt be snapped up as teachers in some dreadful inner London Secondary Modern institution of the British education system.

It was then with some sadness that we said farewell to the College and its superior landlord, the University. The Drinking Set hired a local hall and everyone was invited to toast the old Alma Mater with as much beer, sordid jokes and as many of Barry Humphries' double-entendre songs as could fit in before we were all tossed out. Before this happened, we had toasted all of our lecturers, several of who were in attendance and decided to change the College's motto to 'infectum in lucem' – which could be as loosely translated as 'wet light' which seemed to be appropriate at the time.

Chapter Three: Practice Makes Perfect

The old train rattled on. The landscape had become flatter, dryer and browner. There were still a few trees here and there; small copses where farmers had been unable to remove them because of stony ground. The highway occasionally ran up close to the line like some giant bitumen-black snake. Its few vehicles flashing past as if to mock the slow speed of our glorious express.

I had become bored with my long journey. The dusty water still washed back and forth in the dirty carafe held in its tarnished metal holders bolted near the ceiling, the small fly-blown electric fans still hung lifeless and limp in the ceiling and the long strands of yellow fly-paper still hung above the doorways with their forlorn remnants of victims long past. The excitement which I had experienced at the beginning of my expedition into the new world of First Appointment - Country Service had started to wear off. Some apprehension about my future ability began to creep into my thoughts like the darkness of dusk creeping down the long corridor at home in the small, semi-detached cottage which I had shared with my mother and father only yesterday. Was I good enough to be a real teacher? I had been well-trained but could I put all of those new ideas in practice when I stood alone and without any support in a class of forty or so potential trouble-makers?

These fears brought back my memories of my only previous brief encounters with real life in the classroom. Twice every year, the College had sent out its innocent neophytes to selected schools in periods of terror, trial and error and mayhem called 'Practice Teaching'. With some rare understanding of the practical needs of its students, the College always attempted to send their inmates to schools near their own home. This familiarity was meant to instil some home-friendly feelings of comfort as well as to alleviate the burden of public transport.

My first school was Southside Intermediate Technical High School: a name which some of its more challenged students found difficult to complete, so they usually just called it 'Tech High' or 'Southy' for short. It was a mark of some honour to be a member of this establishment and the older boys used the term in a gangland context and often demonstrated their school culture by bullying any private school students found on the street or on any shared public buses. All students from this school would leave after gaining their 'Inter', or not, at age fifteen and go into the trades, or generally get a job or just become unemployed. Some whom had had difficulties with their studies and were made to repeat a year or two usually left at a much older age or left at fifteen anyway, having realised that school was not for them. This had been the usual schooling for most boys and girls in the state ever since schooling was made compulsory in the nineteenth century. Out in the country, from where my parents had migrated during the Great Depression, few students went past the traditional leaving age of fifteen and my stepfather had left the farm at age twelve to work on the roads with the Main Roads Department. There was always plenty of work around for strong lads, and most girls retreated into 'home duties' assisting their mothers until it was their time to snare some unexpecting male, get married and start the cycle of birth, school and the real world all over again.

Tech High was going to be my first introduction to the real world of teaching. My previous concept of teaching came only from my interaction, good or bad, from my own schooldays and from the observation of the exemplar teachers during our few College 'Observation Lessons' on some of our 'free Fridays'. Teaching from this staged perspective looked good and the classroom environment of these schools and the comfortable teaching styles of these experienced professionals gave me an impression of happy interaction, short working hours, indoor comfort, long holidays and I assumed good pay. Those ideas were to change or at best be greatly modified.

Tech High was also convenient in that it was just across the street from my home of some seventeen years. Most of my early boyhood friends had passed through the school and had left only just over two years previously to go into the trades, banks or offices. I also knew the area well and had a good understanding of the type of teenager who lived in our suburb after all, I was still one of them. The Sydney suburb of Southside was a place for the average working man but one which I remembered with some affection. Our street, which had a row of semi-detached brick building on one side and the school on the other, had been a housing development which had quickly sprung up during the mid-1940's. The twin construction of two brick house sharing a common central wall was the main theme throughout the whole suburb. Most of the people living here worked in the nearby industrial estates further west and south around the big expanse of Botany Bay. My father was now a maintenance painter at the local power station and our neighbours were a tight-knit group of friends who worked in the local penitentiary as warders, or were policemen, stevedores or tradies. It was a tough neighbourhood but there was little local crime in our street for some unknown reason.

In the first 'pract' session, student teachers were usually assigned to one, or perhaps two 'Master Teachers' and would be expected to do mostly observations of the designated guru(s) with perhaps a few very guided upfront lessons with the teacher sitting in. In my first encounter of the first kind, I was simply handed the full timetable and roll of the classroom teacher for three of his classes by my guru, the Head of Science. He was one of the 'old school' who came up through the ranks of Two-year trained (Non-graduate) teachers who had been finally given promotion after many failed attempts and now was somewhere near retirement age. He was a stocky, unkept looking man with a big beer gut which usually poked out from a dirty shirt and a grubby tie which displayed what he had had for breakfast that morning. The boys called him 'Old Bill' and it was difficult to think of him as Mr. Masters, Master Teacher. I was given a Form II class and two Form III classes to practice on and was also required to watch some of 'Old Bill's other classes as well. In addition, I was also assigned to assist him stopping brawls during his supervision of the Wednesday afternoon Rugby matches. There was also the mandatory 'playground supervision' during two lunch hours per week.

Before describing the perils of doing playground supervision in a tough school where anything could happen during lunch breaks and usually did, I must mention 'King'. He was the 'school dog'. In these days, pet dogs were allowed to roam the streets and King was the top dog in the neighbourhood. He was a large part Alsatian – Golden Collie and had all of the long-haired features of a collie but with a much bigger frame and shorter nose. He was a very friendly and intelligent dog and also happened to be my personal pet and childhood companion. My father had brought him home as a small pup and he was raised to be my constant companion and protector. In my primary school days, he also helped my best friend and I do the local paper route on Sundays delivering the newspapers so he was well-known to all in the neighbourhood. He had followed my best friend when he went to Southy and I took off for more distant Madgewick. Naturally King became the school dog and was tolerated by the school staff.

It was my first day of playground supervision. Perhaps 'playground' was a poor use of a term as it was more akin to no man's land at the Somme than a mere playground! Only the barb wire, trenches and shooting were absent but I am sure that the Department would have installed the first two if the shooting had started. I wandered up and down and around corners of various buildings trying to look older than my seventeen years and with an air of confident security. The students seemed to be generally tolerant of student teachers, after all they all knew that I was not a 'real' teacher and had more important things to do such as eating, playing cards and standing over younger boys for their lunch money. Suddenly a large, raucous crowd developed over on the other side of the grassy playground.

"Sir, sir. Come quickly!" a small Form II urchin from my newly-acquired class cried, rushing up and pointing towards the crowd which by now had attracted every boy available. At the time I did not know that I was being set up, as the urchin was the flunky of a gang of Form III boys who ruled the playground. Innocently I rushed up to the crowd and pushed my way through. I should have known what was going on by the sideways knowing glances, winks and smirks on several of the tougher faces.

"Sir!" one of the ring leaders yelled, grabbing my arm and helping me through the multitude "a vicious dog has dug up the pigs head that Old Bill had buried to get its skull for biology and it won't let us near it!"

Breaking into the eye of the storm, there certainly was a large dog baring its teeth and keeping all at bay with the occasional snarl. It had indeed dug up Old Bill's pig's head and guarded it with considerable aggression. It was also my dog King.

"Make room!" I cried. "What a bunch of pansies you all are, being afraid of a mere dog!" I continued with a great show of bravado. I went over to King who jumped up and wagged his tail.

"Clear the area!" I commanded, giving King a well-deserved pat on the head. "And bury that revolting head!" I added to the toughest group of louts who stood gasping with their mouths open in total disbelief in my ability to handle wild dogs.

"Ooooh!" they collectively said and pushed the head back into its sandy hole.

King went home at my command and I continued on with my patrol confident now that I had gained a great deal of 'street cred' with the boys. Small groups of gamblers and bullies suddenly split up every time I came around the corner.

This act of 'bravery' against a vicous animal soon got around the school and coupled with Old Bill's unique discipline device, I had no trouble with my classes. On the first day, Old Bill had told me the secret of his discipline by taking me into the preparation room which led off from the Form III classroom.

"If any of the little bastards look like giving me any crap, I take 'em in 'ere and show 'em this." He bragged. 'This' was his 'discipline device' and was a long metal vat filled with linseed oil which Old Bill had used during the Cricket season. In the vat was the biggest and thickest cane – sorry, 'pointer stick' in official Departmental terms – that I had ever seen.

"I tells 'em that they are going to be the first to test this beauty and they all get the message. Understand?" said the sage.

I understood perfectly. Watching Old Bill perform in class I knew that his threat about his 'beauty' was a well-known old tale handed down as part of the legends of the school and that the real secret of Bill's discipline was his good relationship with the boys. They loved his act of a tough exterior and would show appropriate 'fear' if they were shown 'The Vat' as they called it. I doubt that the cane had ever came out of its trough of oil in the many years that 'Old Bill' had been at that school.

The other eccentricity that Old Bill was known for was the 'High Drop'. Our room was on the second story above a quadrangle paved in bitumen. In these days, most boys from tech High carried what were known as 'airways bags' – long, soft bags which could be carried over their shoulders by a long strap. Bags were not permitted in the laboratory because of safety Bill had told me, but it also was to prevent theft of laboratory equipment and chemicals which the boys could then make into explosives. Amateurs! I thought. I was sometimes tempted to stop my prepared lesson on such interesting topics as the sex life of warty newts and give them all a lesson from an expert. Smuggling items out of the laboratory had been my forte at my old school and Teachers College had not dimmed my personal love of chemicals and other scientific wonders. However, now I had gone from making explosive 'touch powder' to smear on classroom door handles to making rockets which my old friend Petros and I would launch out in the country on weekends.

Bill's 'High Drop' was his attempt to get the boys to neatly place their bags along the wall in the corridor outside the laboratory. This was the equivalent of making any teenager keep their bedroom clean and tidy, to wash their hands and call their mother 'mater'. It simply did not work until Bill got the great idea for his 'High Drop'. He would huff and puff along the corridor after the boys had entered his classroom and then take the bags lying in the middle of the corridor and hang them out of the window. He would pull down the window so that its fame jammed the strap of the bag, preventing it from falling. After the lesson was over and the inmates came out to take up their bags, those who had offended Old Bill saw their bags hanging outside the window. The dullest students would lift up the window and watch their bag plummet to the ground. The next group of non-intellectuals would do nothing and have to go to the next class where they would be punished for not having their books which were still in their bags hanging from the window. A small group of students with more sense and who would probably go on to become leaders of local gangs, would work as a team with one going downstairs to catch the plummeting bags once released.

The rest of my Practice Teaching sessions were much less stressful than my first but never-the-less taught me some of the finer points of classroom teaching. They also taught me about how teachers really behaved behind the scenes and how to relate to the students. No end of information from our Psychology and Teaching Methods lecturers from College could teach us about the personal dynamics between a teacher and their own class.

My next school was even further south from my home and deeper into the city's more historically primitive areas. It was another industrial area which also bordered one of the First Nation's tribal territories which had long since been overrun by the fringes of the city and its white inhabitants. The power station where my father worked in maintenance, was just down the road on the shores of

Botany Bay, and the local penitentiary which had a tough reputation, was immediately across the road from the school. This school was one of the newer institutions and went to Year 12, the name changing from Form V, and the students sat for the external Leaving Certificate at the end of their final year. The two senior years, not being part of compulsory education, were small as most of the students left at fifteen to go into trades, become shop-assistants or go on the dole. Of the latter group, a small number found their way in the 'house of correction' across the road.

My stay at this school was quite pleasant. As well as junior science classes, I also got to teach Senior Physics despite my feeble plea that I was only a trainee junior secondary teacher. My supervising teacher only laughed at this and gave me some good advice:

"Listen, young Mr Shipley, to the Department you are a teacher and therefore can teach anything, including Senior Physics. They are so short of science teachers that you will probably be teaching more senior classes than junior."

As it eventuated, he was right and I did end up teaching all of the senior sciences as well as mathematics, engineering, physical education, music and some other subjects on a more temporary basis.

Although Botany Bay High School was considered a tough school, and such rumours were eagerly shared around the College once our 'choice' of schools had been allocated, I again had some good luck and so my discipline was good enough to allow me to survive and get on experimenting with teaching my new classes. I was especially certain about teaching Heisenberg's Uncertainty Principle to the Senior Physics class, even if they had their own uncertainties as to what it all meant.

My new found aura of discipline came during one playground supervision session. The school was fairly modern and to give the teachers on patrol some extra security, an above-ground catwalk had been erected on top of a walkway between two of the main buildings. This became somewhat of a joke amongst both students and teachers alike as within plain view just across the road was the forbidding walls of the penitentiary with its own catwalk high up on its walls. It was not uncommon for a patrolling teacher to return the bored wave from on of the guards at the other institution across the road. This often was given with the understanding that some of our graduates would end up across the road in the very near future. The joke went around the staff that we were really just a junior annex of the penitentiary across the road.

On that day, I had declined the catwalk and had come down to earth to see what the students were up to. The girls were generally a quiet bunch and did not want to interact with this strange new being who had descended upon them. The boys were generally disinterested and were more content with eating their lunch, gambling or extorting lunch money from the younger boys. Suddenly I was confronted by a huge boy from my Year 10 class. He was of the local First Nation tribe and was both taller and broader than I. Moreover, the shape of his nose and the toughness of skin suggested that he was a tough customer indeed and had been in many brawls.

"You Big Vic's son?" he challenged. I was taken aback by hearing my father's nick name which was often used by his friends in our street.

"Umm,…yes." Was all that would come out of my open mouth as I looked up into his rather stern black face and his dull, insensitive eyes. What was going to happen next, I thought. There was not another teacher in sight and the students all suddenly seemed to be occupied with other things with faces turned away from this confrontation. The air had suddenly gone very still and cold.

"Yeah! 'e works with my dad an' he's a good mate, see? You're one of us now Bro. and we will look afta ya!" He said with a broad grin which cracked his face almost in two and he turned away and ambled off. I stood there a while as my shock disappeared and I returned to some normality. My father, I thought was a great man. He often brought some of his workmates home for an afternoon beer or two, and having the experience of working on many docks on the waterfront in his youth, he saw everyone as a friend regardless of their race, religion or colour until proven otherwise. This was his governing philosophy and whilst he rarely gave me family talks on such matters, the lessons had gone home.

My supervisor from the College had been Mr. Wells who watched my teaching style with some objectivity and patiently listened to my rantings about my educational philosophy of predestination with some tolerance - well, until we met again unexpectedly in my second year.

As fate would have it, my third session of inflicting my neophyte skills and developing personal style on hapless children, was at my old school, Madgewick High. It was at the beginning of my second year at the College but I returned to my old school with great trepidation. I was uncomfortable in my shabby suit and non-matching tie and now felt out of place that I was back here and not in my old school uniform. I also was embarrassed to see that the Russian flag which my fellows and I of the departing

Senior Year had cemented onto the roof of the History Block was still there. It had fallen over and the red was badly faded but it was still flying defiantly as no one had bothered to climb up and take it down, least of all Mr. Dominic. It had been less than two years ago that this 'flag-raising' had occurred and we had got away with it only because the main focus of attention of the Headmaster and the few staff who cared about such puerile trivia, had been the main school flagpole. Departing Seniors had had a tradition of hauling various items up this flagpole so that they would be in full view of the assembled school and the main road which ran past the school into the city. Pirate flags, a collection of ladies' underwear and at some rare times even an effigy of the Headmaster would often be strung up. Our small departing gift was more a tribute our history teacher, Mr Dominic than a puerile protest about twelve years of schooling.

The current staff at Madgewick were somewhat startled in an incredulous way, that one of their recent ejects should suddenly show up in their midst and in the staff common room. I also felt uncomfortable here as well, but luckily my supervising teacher was 'Dud' Dudley, my old chemistry teacher, who had luckily forgotten that I had once been one of his students much to my relief. So my presence was begrudgingly accepted, especially by some of my former teachers who thought that I had been relatively harmless and at least a good average student. Mr Smith my Greek-looking former teacher of BP and A, gave me a friendly welcome with the comment that I would never had made a good accountant anyway as I never did know whether debit was on the left and credit on the right. I was, however disappointed that the school had now employed a professional Laboratory Manager and that Madgewick's incumbent was an older lady who always kept an eagle eye on every test-tube and grain of potential explosive in the storeroom. From now on, I would be issued with extremely minimal amounts of any equipment, but especially anything which might have some interesting potential. In her mind, student teachers were more dangerous than Year 12 students and should not be allowed to handle anything other than that a five-year-old child might find hazardous. Perhaps she was right!

My time at Madgewick was relatively boring when compared to my days there as a student. There were no practical jokes, bully-baiting and certainly no explosions. Only on one occasion was there a glimmer of my past life. I was programmed to teach the reaction of acids on sulfide compounds in a Year 11 Chemistry class. The Guardian Valkyrie of the preparation room had issued me with the standard microscopic piece of iron sulphide which I was to drop into a long test-tube to which a little sulfuric acid was to be cautiously added. This would produce some fizzing as poisonous hydrogen sulfide gas was given off. The test-tube could then be safety passed around the room so that the students should also cautiously smell this totally obnoxiously-smelling gas which lay at the bottom of the test-tube. This is the same gas which comes from uncleaned drainage pipes and sewers.

Being a former Laboratory Prefect in this very school, I had known where the bottle of iron sulfide was kept and this very reaction had been one, which I as a student, had often used to clear the smokers out of their toilet habitats. Seeing that the Keeper of All Things Nasty had left the room, and that Dud had been momentarily been called away. I quickly dashed into the preparation room and purloined the said bottle.

"Go on, Sir, put a bigger piece in!" was the assembled cry from the class when I returned triumphantly with the bottle.

"OK. Stand back!" I exclaimed and dropped a bigger piece of iron sulfide into a bigger test-tube followed by a more generous amount of acid. It fizzed remarkably well, with the mixture rising up out of the test-tube, over the wooden test-tube rack and onto the desk. The volume of gas was incredible for such a small amount of reactant and the gas soon filled the front of the laboratory with an incredibly odorous smell. I was rather startled at this sudden evidence of my nefarious activity but was soon gratified as most of the boys in the front row had collectively reached for their school hats and were fanning the gas away from the front bench. Others had quickly closed the classroom door and another group had opened all of the windows.

"Don't worry, Sir. We'll take the blame!" they cried. What a group of gentlemen the school was still producing! I quickly returned the bottle to its dusty space in the preparation room and put the offending test-tube in the fume hood to live out its brief, but smelly life. Having done this, I resumed my teaching as though nothing untoward had happened.

Upon returning to the classroom, Dud was happy to see a quiet group of boys busily copying up the notes for the demonstration and his student teacher at the front desk still intact; the smell having faded to just a faint trace of its former malodour.

"What's that smell, Mr. Shipley? He asked. "It smells like hydrogen sulfide gas."

"It's the experiment Mr. Dudley." I replied in all innocence and he shuffled back to the rear of the laboratory to once again resume his observations out the open window. Later he expressed his apologies in leaving me to handle such a dangerous experiment and expressed supreme confidence in my future abilities. The boys worked on with quiet smiles on their faces.

My last practice school highlighted the problem of being a young teacher in a local school. The school was another of the new generation of coeducational senior-year high schools. This was located only a short distance from the main beach where my friends and I would surf at the weekends. It was sometimes difficult to stop my students gazing out of the windows looking at the set of the waves on a good day.

"The surf's up" someone would say and then attention towards the blackboard would cease until some form of discipline would be imposed. This would soon also fly out of the window because I too would go over and look at the waves. "Surf's up" I would think and look at the classroom clock estimating how many hours it would be until I too could hit the water and what the tide would be like at that time.

This was a new school and I was now a mature age College student of almost nineteen. Before this school had opened at the start of this year, boys from this suburb would have gone to the next nearest boys' high school which was Madgewick, so many of the names of my students were familiar to me as they were the same as some of my friends from school. Older brothers no doubt. One day, one of the girls in my Senior Biology class, who had been obviously doing some quick arithmetic and genealogy in her head, suddenly blurted out:

"You went to school with my brother! He's only eighteen!"

This was the great revelation to the other students, especially the girls who suddenly realised that the shy young man standing in front of them was also only of this vintage. Some of these 'young ladies' were in fact only a year or two younger than I and certainly had a great deal more development. Discipline tumbled for a moment as I confessed the truth but explained that I was still their teacher and lied about the tremendous power I possessed over their young lives. That statement of course was totally ignored but they were a decent class so they accepted me at least as someone who knew a little more biology than they did. Well, 'little' was the operating word here.

My classroom relationships and teaching at this stage was not the main problem. That came on the very next Saturday when I was again down on the beach with my friends sitting on the sand waiting for the waves to pick up.

"Hello Sir," said a feminine voice from behind me as some of my senior girls walked past in their bikinis. They were quite attractive out of uniform but the College had instilled us with an almost paranoid fear of getting involved with students of the opposite sex. All I could do was to raise my hand in a mild acknowledgement of their greeting and a rather shy smile. My friends, however, showed all of the signs of rampant teenage enthusiasm and made appropriate male gestures and comments typical of the 1960's. No, I would not hand out lists of names and addresses and almost felt a fatherly sense of protection. After all, I knew exactly what my friends were like and I had to face these girls on Monday.

Back at school, I tried to keep a very low profile in the playground and a falsely stern attitude in class, especially in my Senior Biology class. The girls were good sports and apart from the usual knowing smile and coming a little bit closer than usual, things returned to normal. I was shy and they knew it.

My enthusiasm for all things new and science in particular almost became my undoing in this school. Teaching about air pressure to my junior class, I got the uninformed idea of how to boil water under reduced pressure and at a low temperature. In the preparation room, I had boiled a little water in a triangular glass flask. Having driven all of the air out, I rammed a rubber stopper tightly into its mouth and waited until the steam condensed. This would create a near vacuum in the flask. I enthusiastically rushed into the nearby science staffroom where several of the older teachers were quietly working.

"Look!" I said. "I can boil this water with only the warmth of my hand!" I held the bottom of the flask in my hand and waited for the water to boil. Nothing happened. I was determined to show that I could boil water at a low temperature so, grabbing a box of matches from one of the desks, I struck the match and held it to the base of the flask. There was a very loud 'bang' as the flask imploded with great force sending fragments of glass, water and small patches of blood (mine!) over the teachers and their notebooks. There was a sudden outcry of mixed derision and shock and a few enquiries about my welfare. I was quickly bundled out of the room by the Head of Science whist my unfortunate colleagues cleaned up the mess. Unconcerned about my welfare he gave me a quick lesson in how I should have used a round-bottomed flask and cork stopper for such an experiment. Despite my enthusiastic stupidity, my supervising teacher gave me a satisfactory grade for my other activities.

Practice Teaching had been a series of both fortunate and unfortunate events. I had learned a lot from some great teachers who had the tolerance and professionalism to pass on their knowledge and a little of their personalities to this enthusiastic but naïve creature who was now being released as a fully-trained Junior Secondary Science Probational Teacher (non-graduate).

Chapter Four: First Contact

It was late in the afternoon by the time our tired old express pulled itself slowly into the station that was the end of the line: Canberra the nation's capital. The carriages came to a shuddering halt and the water in the dusty old carafes ceased its weary oscillations. The flypaper hung limp above the door as the few weary passengers in the carriage stood and stretched their aching limbs. I reached up and hauled down my battered old cardboard suitcase which had belonged to my grandfather, and shuffled off down the central aisle with my fellow inmates. I was tempted to put up one hand on the shoulder in front of me and keep my eyes downcast but got over it. It had been a long six-hour journey and I was sure that had we been boarded by the Wild Bunch, Butch Cassidy, or Ned Kelly and his gang of bushrangers, that my fellow passengers would have welcomed them with open arms as a blessed relief from the monotonous boredom of Government Rail.

The platform was uninviting. Bare, sterile, cold and smelling of diesel fumes from our worn out express. No doubt it met all of the Public Service requirements for a Government Issue station: Railway Station - persons for the use of. There was no welcome here! There were a few people being welcomed by their love ones but they had alighted mainly from the First-Class carriages. We minions from Second Class had no one to greet us and we were but a handful. I doubt that any higher-level Public Servant nor politician went by train; they would have travelled by air and landed at the airport not too far away. It was shared with the local Air Force base just in case these dignitaries needed protection; probably from revolutionaries from the National Capital Express.

The second thing which I noticed after the sterility and relative emptiness of the station, was the coolness of the air. Perhaps this also was a requirement of Government Rail stations but most likely because the Capital was situated at two thousand feet above sea level and set well inland from the moderating influences of the sea.

Picking up my poor old suitcase, I trudged along the platform and out into the open spaces of the car park. This seemed to extend out into the even wider expanses of the Australian bush as the station was set, like the airport, well away from the city. The surrounding hills were generally brown with only a scattering of low gum trees. The air was crystal clear and one could see for miles if one had the inclination to see more of the same dull panorama extending off into the distant horizon. There was no evidence of any public transportation to go into the city. No buses to take the happy throng from their escape from the train; no greeting from any representatives from the

Education Department welcoming its new bringer of the Light of Science to this cheerless place. There was, however a taxi rank with two drab cabs with their tired occupants sitting uninvitingly at the curb waiting for someone to ask their drivers for their favour should they feel like accepting a fare. I summoned up the last of my enthusiasm and walked up to the first cab. By an automatic response which seemed to be in slow motion, the driver reluctantly put down his newspaper and climbed out of his cab, threw his cigarette butt to the ground and raised the boot of his cab. He picked up my tired old cardboard suitcase and threw it unceremoniously into the back of his cab and slammed the boot lid shut.

"Where to, mate?" he said with a tone that showed no sign of interest.

"Capital House." I replied and climbed into the rear of the cab.

It was a short drive into the city, passing the small area which was quietly referred to by the locals in hushed tones as 'the industrial estate'. This consisted of a few streets of low sheds and yards which clustered together like poor orphans which had been ejected from the garden opulence of the city which refused to admit to any such 'working class' presence. These disgraced buildings soon passed by and the manicured and well-kept lawns and gardens of Canberra now began to present themselves. Things were starting to look up. The roads became dual-lane highways and the suburban streets were lined with neat, single story houses or even neater two-story blocks of units. There was a similarity in the architecture and beautification of each street which suggested a planned uniformity of the nation's capital. No slums nor poorly-kept rental houses here!

I was looking forward now to my accommodation as the sun had started to set over the blue-hued mountain to the west and the long travel exposed to toxic diesel fumes and dust had finally taken their toll. In such a planned and neatly coiffured city, my anticipation of luxury at Capital House seemed assured. A brochure had come with my letter of First Appointment; along with my letter of appointment and my Second-Class rail ticket aboard the grand National Capital Express. This brochure, in glorious black and white explained that Capital House was a Government Hostel of superior quality providing all of its well-appointed amenities at full board. The implication was that any newly-arrived Public Servant would be well looked after in the manner that was appropriate for such worthies. There was a photograph on the front cover showing a low-lying, collection of single-story buildings. The centre was occupied by a long block fronted by a wide veranda and approached via a paved avenue flanked with tall trees and spacious lawns. On either side of this building and set at right-angles to it, were several long accommodation blocks. The whole effect of this photograph conjured up a vision of some well-run country club where minions of the Government could relax or play at their leisure in true comfort befitting servants of the Public.

The cab stopped with a sudden jerk indicating that we had arrived. I gave the cabbie the appropriate fare, which seemed rather severe compared to my limited knowledge of my home city's equivalent, and climbed out. It is amazing how photographs can be taken to give a false impression. No doubt it was taken by a professional; photographer who spent most of his time taking photographs for real estate companies, land developers and media personalities who had long since passed their 'use-by date'!

The wide lawns and extensive gardens now seemed to be a lot smaller and more of a brown colour with patches of bare dirt showing through what at better times would be called 'lawn'. At least the long 'tree-lined' avenue was a lot shorter but the main building had a sad look about it. It was a timber structure with a corrugated iron roof showing patches of rust here and there. Perhaps once it might have been painted a brilliant white, but now the colour seemed to have faded to a dull, blotchy cream and in places the paint had fallen off the timber entirely. To add to the depressing scene in front of me, the cabbie had once again thrown my precious old suitcase, this time onto the curb. Could this be a new sporting event for some bizarre 'Cabbie Olympics'? Hitting the ground, the tired old catches of my suitcase popped open, strewing some of my meagre belongings onto the dry grass. The cabbie Olympian eased his fat body back into his cab and drove off leaving me to take in the surroundings of my open suitcase and the drab buildings in front of me. Oh well! At least I didn't have to find my own accommodation and the brochure had bragged that 'all meals, including cut lunches would be provided'.

I sorted out my clothing and packed it back into the suitcase which I was lucky enough to close. Mounting the unpainted and worn wooden steps, I entered the main office through a set of double wooden doors. There was a long, wooden bench running the entire length of this room with various faded travel posters on the wall behind. Perhaps they were there to give an international and worldly feel to the place. Once perhaps.

A middle-aged office girl stared at me blankly from across the counter. No welcoming smile nor cheerful 'good afternoon' here! To break the silence, I stammered out something like my name and the obvious fact that accommodation had been arranged for me here.

 Miss Congeniality gave me another stare and pushed a piece of paper which I was to sign with the pen sitting limply in a holder nearby. There was also another document bearing yet another glorious photograph of the establishment with the threatening title of 'Rules and Regulations for the Happiness of Guests'.

"Room E10. Out the door, turn left and take the second corridor to the right" came the monotone of my new acquaintance. With that she turned and got on with the more important task of dusting off the travel posters on the wall behind.

Accordingly, like the new servant of the Public which I had now become, I went out of the door, turned left along the veranda and walked past the first block which ran in both directions at right angles to the veranda until I came to the second block beyond. I turned dutifully to the right and looked down the corridor which was part of the romantically-named 'E-block'. Had Ned Kelly and his gang once been incarcerated within these walls? Most unlikely considering the construction of the buildings which reminded me of the barracks I had seen in prisoner-of-war movies of more recent vintage. The long passageway extended both in front and behind me as a very narrow corridor with a central strip of faded, floral linoleum underfoot. Both walls on either side were painted in a dull, light green colour and had doors set into them which obviously were the cells of other inmates. Above each door was an electrical power meter which would monitor any excessive use of power which the inmates may use and which would be added to their account each fortnight.

Cautiously I opened the wooden door which had been marked as 'E10'. It was, as I had guessed from the close proximity of the doors along the corridor, a small room. It was lined with cheap fibre board and painted in the same dull, light green colour. 'Economy of scale' Mr. Greek Smith of BP and A would have said of the tendency of Government constructions to be painted 'en masse'. At least it wasn't 'Battleship Grey!

There was a small window in the wall opposite the door and this had a fly-blown brown roller blind and was surrounded by a limp, thread-bare lace curtain. There was a single light bulb hanging from the ceiling decorated with a small, meaningless conical plastic lampshade. Well, at least it seemed clean and would keep the weather at bay.

Furniture was minimal; a single iron-framed bed with thin Government Issue mattress, a large old wardrobe with peeling varnish, a small wooden desk and chair and a waste paper basket. The floor was covered with the ubiquitous faded floral linoleum but there was a small brown mat which had seen generations of boots and cigarettes. I put my suitcase down and sat on the bed wondering what disappointment would come next.

It came whilst I further explored the amenities of my new abode. Toilets and showers were in a central room in the middle of the long E Block and consisted of wooden partitions and doors which only went halfway to the ceiling and started about a foot from the bare and rough-cast concrete floor below. The tops of the outer walls also did not quite make the ceiling; perhaps there were cutbacks in Government spending when these blocks were being constructed. At present they allowed a good flow of dry air through the room, but in winter it would be a different story. At least there was a good supply of very hot water provided by a small boiler house set behind the buildings. Toilet cubicles were similarly constructed and aerated. Personal washing facilities for clothing consisted of old concrete tubs arranged along one wall and there was a large, round 'copper' or circular metal tub the outside of which was serviced by a steam pipe from the boiler house and surmounted by a mechanical mangle which would be used to squeeze out water from the boiled clothing. I had not seen such facilities since my mother had taken me to Great Aunt Tilly's country farm in the 1950's.

The rest of the afternoon was spent in unpacking my bag and rearranging my things in the old wardrobe which creaked sadly every time I opened one of the doors or drawers. This finished, I sat and stared at the faded green walls until the promised 'Dinner at six o'clock sharp – no late comers allowed!'

Dinner was both a disappointment and a lift in my spirits. Naturally, according to the rules, I had been allocated a table which seated five other hungry souls. A sign bearing a large pointing hand and the words 'queue here' put me in the right direction for the food servery and I joined a long line of other hungry inmates. Again, the image of a prison line drifted into my tired head but again I got over the urge to put one hand up on the shoulder in front of me. This being a Sunday, the fare for the evening was the usual roast with baked vegetables. I like a roast dinner and the blackboard above the servery proclaimed that the 'Menu du jour' was a pretentious 'Boeuf à façon du pays, haricots verts pommes vapeur' which my schoolboy French suggested that it was a roast beef baked dinner. The cultured words on the blackboard seemed to be at odds with the large packed hall of basic plastic-topped tables and chairs and the general air of mass production and noisy eating not to mention the food which was very average and demonstrated the chef's ability to destroy a standard Sunday roast.

I pushed my metal tray along the railing in front of the servery and past the serving staff who unceremoniously slopped the food onto a large white plate embossed with the nation's coat of arms. The staff seemed to be as disinterested in their work as the girl on the desk at my first encounter. Perhaps there was a special training course somewhere for front desk public servants and cooks. The food appeared to be rather bland and looked as though it had been prepared in bulk many hours beforehand; as indeed it had.

I wondered through the crowded hall until I found a table with my allocated number sticking up from a small metal stand and sat down.

"Gidday, Hairy legs." Said the scruffy, black-bearded apparition at the other end of the table. Perhaps Ned Kelly and his gang of train-robbers had been here all of the time. He introduced himself and the rest of his gang who sat around the table. They were a mixed breed of guys about my age and all passed their hands across the table in welcome.

"Well, another poor wretch sentenced to life in Stalag 13!" said Ned Kelly cheerfully, his mouth showing gaps where a few teeth were missing and the others to be stained with tobacco juice as was his beard. Ned went by the pseudonym of 'Jacko' and was obviously the top personality of the table. I confessed to my new arrival and lack of joy at the deceptive nature of Capital House's brochure. Universal laughter came from my new friends.

"No problems," said Ron who sat at my elbow. "We all had that shock! But one gets used to it and we make our own fun around here. You'll like it!" he promised. Dinner progressed with much animated talk and I soon found that my new friends were an open and happy, though somewhat unconventional bunch. As luck would have it, the mysterious cogwheels of the Public Service had unknowingly allocated me to a table which would be described in their dull terms as 'misfits'. Most worked for government agencies which, like mine, were not linked to the usual hierarchy of the Commonwealth Public Service. Only Will was a 'real' Public Servant but he didn't say much and had easily been converted to the ideals of his fellow diners who saw the rest of the inhabitants here as targets for practical jokes.

"They need to get a life!" Jacko had explained because "the poor bastards spend all day pushing paper about."

He and the others suggested that we all repair to the local hotel and continue with a liquid desert in lieu of the weak custard and tinned fruit on offer in the dining room. Unfortunately, and very reluctantly I put this offer on hold because I still had to sort myself out as tomorrow would be a big day.

"Such is life!" said Jacko as I made my departure. Perhaps I was wrong about Ned Kelly after all but now I felt that I had finally arrived.

I had made enquiries at dinner about where my new school was located and how to get there. The front lady at the office slapped a map onto the counter and pointed with a pudgy finger the location of my new school. West Capital High School was apparently a new school built on the outskirts of the then known civilized world, or at least what the public servants called anywhere outside of the city's administrative precinct.

"Jeez!" said Will. "That's miles away out near the scrub!" Will's Public Servant's mentality sometimes broke through his usual silence when some new and interesting event passed his way.

"No worries, Hairy Legs." Said Jacko. He called most people 'Hairy Legs' and it was be considered a term of endearment. Now, to be called 'Dog's Breath' was another matter. It was usually said with a hostile sneer and often meant trouble.

Jacko explained that the public transport system in Canberra left a lot to be desired. This meant that walking was often the best and sometimes only option. In my case unfortunately, the school was at least six miles away in one of the new, outer suburbs 'out near the scrub'. Jacko, luckily knew the area well. He was a surveyor's field assistant for a QANGO or quasi-autonomous non-governmental organisation; an organisation to which the government had devolved power, but which still partly controlled its finances. This meant that Jacko could not be equated to most other public servants when he socialised. This became apparent later at parties of the lowly pimpled-face set which comprised most of the city's younger public servants. Usually, some three-piece suit would amble up with a glass of Chardonnay in its hand and say something in a limp voice such as:

"Hello. I'm Charles and I am a Level 2 in the Department of Administrative Administration what are you?"

If you replied that you were a Level 1 or even a new base-grade clerk then you may be worthy of a few words from Charles; either of encouragement for the future or his commiserations. If you were also a Level 2 then Charles would engage you in almost earnest conversation, taking note of your name and the department in which, you worked. Charles would then certainly look you up as soon as he could in the Commonwealth Gazette to obtain your relative seniority. This was a major and regular habit of such people who would eagerly read this august publication as soon as it hit the office. It would be then thoroughly examined in case one could find the chance to appeal for the better jobs of those of lower rank or seniority when they had achieved a new promotion. However, if you looked down at Charles through half-closed eyes, a haughty stare and a raised eyebrow and loftily proclaimed that you were a Level 3 or higher, Charles would mumble some apology and scurry away. Jacko's response to a Charles introduction would be something like:

"Rack off, Dog's Breath!" I work for the National Survey Organisation – a comment that would leave Charles in a state of confusion, not only about the epithet given to him but also what exactly was the National Survey Organisation. It just did not equate!

Because of his professional wanderings all over the site of the nation's rapidly developing real estate, Jacko knew exactly where the school was located. Afterall, his team had surveyed it late last year and West Capital was a new suburb purpose-built for the public servants and military personnel who worked for the Department of the Army.

"Now, Hairy Legs" my new guru pronounced with just a touch of a homily, "You walk up there to Civic centre to London Circuit, See. An' you find the bus stop to go west and you get the bus to Mitchel. That's almost there. Then you walk about two miles and you're home. Got it?"

That did not sound promising but I believed my benefactor entirely, so I said my farewells and wandered back to my lonely room. There I sorted through my meagre belongings and set out my dark suit, my only suit, my black fish-net tie which was then very trendy and a white shirt. A last polish of my shoes to remove the dust of the National Capital Express and a clean pair of socks and underwear. My briefcase was already packed with the essentials; pen and a thin former school notebook and of course the new Biblical textbook containing everything worth knowing about science and which filled up the rest of the briefcase. All I had to do the next morning was to collect the 'packaged lunch' promised by the chefs of

Capital House after breakfast and then head off to my first day of employment.

Breakfast was a more casual affair than the Sunday Night Roast, although the food was down to its usual mass-produced standard. Dry cereals and various stale bread and cakes were laid out at the beginning of the servery but there was a good choice of hot items along its path. I still cannot understand why the fried eggs were only lightly cooked – 'sunny side up' according to the Americans - and served with indifference off slices of white bread. Perhaps the bread was used as a base to absorb any uncooked egg white? Well as nothing went to waste because of matters of finance rather than conservation, one suspected that the white bread slices went into that evening's 'bread-and-butter pudding' along with the main meal of stew which was the leftovers from the Sunday Night Roast.

I looked into the mysteries of the brown paper bag which had been handed out with the usual indifference by one of the staff near the exit. It contained two sandwiches and a piece of fruit which looked like it came from the reject barrel of the local fruit market. I later found that my firmly wrapped sandwiches consisted of Devon and tomato sauce and another of some sort of orange cheese with salad. The former contained that staple compressed meat of poor Australian households. Totally devoid of flavour and made from the leftovers of meat preparation, it needed something like the ubiquitous tomato sauce to give it some taste. The salad sandwich was a little more nutritious and consisted of a slice of processed orange cheese, one limp lettuce leaf and a slice of tomato. Both sandwiches were on white bread smeared with a microfilm of margarine. Well, at least I did not have to make my own lunch nor spend anything from the small amount of my future wage left over after 'full board' had been extracted at Capital House.

I noticed as I walked up to the bus stop, up the hill towards the city's many concentric circular roads, that there were only a few other commuters. I had left rather early to ensure that I would eventually reach my destination on this first expeditionary sortie, but it appeared that public servants still had plenty of time to reach their hallowed halls. In fact, I later found that many of the younger and female versions were often provided with private car transportation to protect them from the wild men of the Capital. Probably those like Jacko and Ron from the National Survey Organisation, and other QANGOS. Teachers were probably considered to be harmless.

After about an hour's wait the bus for Mitchell finally arrived. Buses only ran every hour or so if they ran at all but they were air-conditioned in summer and heated in winter when the walk to the bus stop was over thick crackling frost or even a light dusting of snow. The bus ride was uneventful as few passengers took this route out into the great unknown which was yet to be fully populated. It ran out along one of the many spokes which radiated out from the even more numerous circles of the capitals inner road system. Occasionally, the bus would turn into one of the outer circles of this maze and pass along newly constructed streets with their newly turfed lawns and newly planted foreign shrubs. The strangeness of this landscape suddenly hit me! There were no front fences for any of the houses which sat exposed to the openness of the road. I was not used to the lack of fences in this city because I was brought up in an older culture where the 'front fence' was part of the street scene and usually a place to join the neighbours for a few beers after work and which had brick letter boxes to be blown up by mischievous teenagers. The well-paved roads abruptly met newly manicured front lawns which ran right up to the doorways and walls of the newly manicured, single storied houses, often all of a similar architecture. It reminded me of the comfortable suburban scene often portrayed in American 'family' programs of the late 1950's. I expected to see wholesome young children pulling their little red wagons and selling lemonade from their soapbox stands with beaming, well-dressed parents looking on from the front porch. But there was no one in the street and it was only the red American-style fire hydrants lining the curb at intervals which reinforced the idea that perhaps I had been somehow transported to 'little America' of past family television. These red fire hydrants later proved to be useful during winter, when the thick morning fogs descended upon the long valley of the capital. They would last all morning and so I would get off my bus and walk along the gutter of the spoke road and navigate with some uncertainty by counting the number of hydrants until I found my destination.

I had no problem in finding my exit bus stop as the shopping centre at Mitchell was the end of the line. I had asked the bus driver when I was alighting the direction to West Capital High School. He sighed and pointed down the long spoke road to which we had returned and now seemed to go off into the early morning scrub of 'terra incognita'.

"About two miles down there, son." He said with a look of commiseration.

The way ahead looked rather desolate apart from the well-paved road which had been put in last year after Jacko and his team had surveyed the area. The air was very clear today with the winds blowing off the distant mountains to the west and southwest. At this time of year and during a drought such as we were now in, the wind from any other direction in summer brought a red brown dust. So, I trudged along with yesterday's dust forming small clouds with every step. My shoes which had received a very earnest polish the night before by now had received a coating of this same red brown dust. Eventually, in the openness of this protosuburb, I saw a collection of closely-spaced and heavily scaffolded buildings. The new West Capital High School was in fact a very large construction site surrounded by small hills of discarded building detritus and the ubiquitous red brown dust.

"What a mess!" I thought as I started my trek up the first hill of debris and dust which separated me from the obvious iron-piped entrance. I felt somewhat like the lost legionnaire Beau Gest of P. C. Wren's famous desert novel of the same name as the red brown dust cloud rose ominously up to my ankles as I trudged along over the dunes.

I was suddenly aware that I was not alone in my desert trek. Of to my right were two more lonely figures battling the sea of mullock heaps. Both men appeared to be older than I and also wore the standard uniform of dark suit with red brown dust up to the ankles. As our tracks finally converged, I put down my briefcase and thrust out my right hand in greeting.

"Gidday! I'm Tom Shipley, the new Science Teacher. Gosh! What a dusty shamble this place is!" I said with my usually open enthusiasm.

The eldest of the two men was tall and well-built. He carried himself with the air of a prize fighter and looked at me with a steady gaze, smiled and replied:

"Good morning, Mr. Shipley. I'm Barry McWhirter the Principal of this 'shambles' and this dusty gentleman next to me is John McIntyre my Deputy."

"Oops!" I though, trying to tug both feet out of my mouth. All I could mumble was a weak "good morning" as I picked up my briefcase and joined by new superiors as we came down out of the desert. Shaking off the red brown dust at the iron scaffolded archway of the main entrance, we entered the clean and open spaces of the entrance hall of West Capital High School. For better or worse and probably the latter, I had made my first contact.

Chapter Five: In at the Deep End

"Staff meeting at nine o'clock sharp, Mr Shipley." Were the parting words from the new leader of me and my fellow desert travellers as we parted at the main door; they to their illustrious executive offices and me to the spacious and empty foyer. I looked around at my newly found oasis. It was indeed impressive and no doubt this was the effect that was intended. The vestibule was in fact, a small covered quadrangle, two stories high with a large white stairway going up to the first floor. I could see that there were classrooms up there which opened out to a wide, white-walled landing which ran all the way around the open space.

The ground floor was covered in very expensive looking linoleum tiles and there was a set of two very large double doors in the wall facing the stairway. The imposing entrance through which the desert trio had walked was actually a mere side doorway. Across from this side door and directly opposite the executive offices, were two laboratories, signified by small windows along the outside upper walls and doors with a small glass window set about head height. There was a third door between these two which did not have a window. This would be the preparation room. Expectantly, I hurried over and tried the first door. It opened and revealed a beautiful school laboratory with a double row of wide, shiny rectangular black laboratory benches complete with sinks with their long, tall goose-neck chrome-plated water outlets and several short, stubby pairs of gas taps. Stacked upon these benches were rows of upside-down laboratory stools. The wall opposite the doorway consisted totally of large glass windows opening out into a large courtyard between this and the next block of cream bricks and glass.

Inside, below the windows was a long bench which ran the entire length of the room. This contained cupboards underneath which were highly-polished sliding wooden doors. The wood was also a light cream colour and the top of the bench was a gleaming black. On my side of the room was a similar long bench and cupboards but above the gleaming black surface was a long wall of buff-coloured corkboard noticeboards and above that the small windows which opened out into the main foyer.

Wow! This was the best laboratory I had ever seen and a fitting venue where I would bring the light of Science to the poor masses of West Capital!

The rear of the room was covered in narrow glass display cabinets with wide glass fronts which could also be slid open. They contained many glass shelves upon which equipment, specimens or other items could be displayed.

The ceiling consisted of white, porous insulating tiles which gave the entire room a clean and professionally scientific appearance.

I turned and looked at the front of the laboratory which would be my sole domain. There was a wide blackboard – painted green, of course – which ran across the front of the room except for two small doors on either side. Near these doors where more notice boards and the teacher's bench was raised on a small stage in front of the blackboard and it too had the usual sink with goose-neck faucet and gas outlets for Bunsen burners. What a great teaching space!

I went into the nearest door in the front of the room. It led into a small black-painted room which had benches around three of the walls with a sink and taps. This was probably a dark room for photographic work and other black arts. A connecting door opened into the preparation room. This was bigger and had many wall cupboards and benches designed to hold all of the necessary chemicals and equipment away from prying eyes and hands. No laboratory prefects for this area I vowed! On one side of this room were more small windows above head height and another closed door. I opened it and went through into a well-lit room which had the wide glass windows of the laboratory extending along its outer wall. On the inner wall were more benches and a large cage with several wide shelves. I could only guess that this was for keeping live animal specimens, something which we had trained for at College but which I had never seen before, having being brought up in the old system of 'boys only' physics and chemistry. The hard realities of teaching practical biology with live animals and all of the attending zoological duties this entailed, began to sink in.

I looked around my potential new domain and felt rather pleased with myself, having become a real teacher and having been appointed to such a pleasant, though sterile city as my 'country service'. I imagined that some of my friends from College were probably still wiping dust from their faces and chasing snakes and kangaroos from their dilapidated schools in their far off 'country service.'

As I surveyed the brand-new desks, the sparkling glass display cases and the freshly laid floor tiles, I realised with a sudden shock that there was something serious wrong with the scene. It was empty of equipment and signs of all of the other paraphernalia needed in bringing the light of Science to the students of West Capital. There were no rows of gleaming glass beakers and flasks in the storage cupboards, no rows of mysterious brown bottles of chemicals, no specimens in the display cases and no orderly rows of textbooks on the shelves. Well, no doubt the new Head of Science would have all of this in hand

and very soon trucks would be arriving to disgorge all of this wonderful scientific bounty.

At ten minutes to nine, I found the new staffroom and sauntered in with the air that this was my natural abode and that my wonderful training and great experience would be instantly recognised by the assembled multitude. There were four people sitting well-spaced around the long, white table which ran down the centre of this bright and airy room. Two looked up at this new apparition which had disturbed their solitude. I sat down in the most vacant area available and mumbled an introduction. Smiles and handshakes followed and we all again settled down to await more newcomers. Within a few minutes there were about twenty of us seated around the table, the end closest to the door had been reserved for the Headmaster and his Deputy as shown by two piles of papers now being rearranged for the umpteenth time by a matronly-looking lady who I surmised was the Head's secretary. Promptly at nine, the two Macs entered and took their seats.

"Welcome to West Capital High," said the Headmaster with a smile which beamed around the room and he introduced his Deputy, John McIntyre who sat dutifully at his elbow. "You may have noticed that it has not yet been finished." He continued. This understatement was received with a few grins from the assembled multitude who still bore the marks of red brown dust around their ankles.

"The Government insisted that we should start a little early." The Headmaster continued. "Unfortunately, construction has been a little slow owing to their expenditure in building the politicians club across the lake. More grins and a few sarcastic comments came from the assembled multitude of twenty.

"However!" he continued. "We have all of the necessary rooms and facilities ready for our students who will be starting next Monday. Two hundred of them to be exact; two classes each of Years Seven and Eight. All we need now is the materials to teach them." The Headmaster shuffled his papers which by now had been well sorted and selected an official piece of paper stamped with a large Government coat of arms.

"Now, let me see who you all are?" he said with another beaming smile. He ran through his staffing lists and received appropriate nods, raised hands and a cough from the worthies whose names were being read out.

Miss Morgenstern was to be Mistress-in-charge of Girls. Whatever that meant! Perhaps she was to be some protector of their morality or pseudo guardian or perhaps even one of those teachers who assumes the guise of Chief Warder and patrols the grounds looking for female offenders to persecute. There was no male equivalent of this role, so I assumed that the boys would have to look after themselves. She certainly looked tough enough for the role and had that grim smile of someone used to power and discipline, often seen only on the faces of Regimental Sergeant Majors on a bad morning.

Mr. Fowles was to be Head of English. He seemed out of place for a literary type and looked as though he would be better placed in a rugby front row. Only his horn-rimmed glasses suggested that he might know something of the Arts. A big man, but one whom I soon found to be a very gentle one and a good friend.

Mr. Withers was Mathematics and he seemed a small, excitable type not used to public scrutiny. I had always been suspicious of mathematics teachers since my old days at school but perhaps Mr Withers deserved the benefit of the doubt as he was a lot younger than the ones I had suffered under.

Miss Greenacre was to be Head of Languages and she beamed back at this pronouncement. She was a rather pretty woman who did not look many years older than I but was, in fact in her mid-twenties and an experienced teacher. An engagement ring on her finger put aside any possible romantic notions on my part and she, like most of my new colleagues was a university graduate.

Mrs. Hughes would be Head of Physical Education and she looked like she could run a marathon before breakfast but gave the Head a very confident nod and looked like she could handle any physical situation.

Mr. Smyth was Head of Woodworking and Metalworking and seemed to be a strong, no-nonsense type who had several years in the Army Engineer Reserves and had 'seen it all before'. Whatever that meant, but it was his favourite saying when something unexpected happened. He was a man of practical wisdom and nothing seem to bother him. When things got tough, he just smiled and gave his other favourite saying 'all extra training value!' which seemed to be appropriate in all very tight circumstances,

The Headmaster rattled off a few names of the other teachers who, like myself were only minions in this organisation. I looked around with some sudden apprehension for a leader in the scientific field. Perhaps someone looking like a cross between Albert Einstein and James Mason, the actor who had played the part of

Professor Lindenbrook in the Disney movie 'Journey to the Center of the Earth'.

The Head broke into my uneasy train of thought. "Ah, Mr Shipley. As there has not been a Head of Science appointed yet due to a clerical error, and you and Miss Higgins are the only representatives of that subject present, you will have to take on the role of Acting Head of the Department of Science. Honorary, of course." With that he pushed several books in my direction which were then passed down the table.

"They are the Order Books for both the Government here and the Education Department back in Sydney. The Government book contains items which are valued at over three hundred pounds and the other has all of the usual paraphernalia which you people need in your laboratory. Will you and Miss Higgins please go through them and order what you think that we will need for your two laboratories. At this stage there is no limit in the expense. Get them back to me tomorrow if you can"

I took the two books and looked at them with feelings of both surprize and wonder. At nineteen years and four months I had the usual concept that I was indestructible, but this new situation rattled my confidence a little.

"Yes, sir." I feebly replied and just sat there looking at the books and wondering what I was to do next. I looked across the table at the Miss Higgins who had shown little life since the beginning of the staff meeting. She was probably a little older than I and looked more like the stereotype spinster librarian than a science teacher. Yet another university graduate with no idea about their future and possible work options. There had been no enthusiasm on her face and certainly the conferring of my acting position as HOD (Science) seemed to be of little consequence to her.

Eventually the meeting closed and the assembled multitude wondered off to search for their new domains amongst their scaffolding and red brown dust. There were a few pats on my back and general comments that I would be alright, especially from those who had no official duties other than to teach their subject under an experienced Head of Department. But then, I was a trained teacher and had been told many times at College that a teacher could do anything. Superman could only leap tall buildings but now I had to find equipment for mine.

As I was leaving, the Head turned and said in an off-hand sort of way "Oh, see me later about the curriculum material. We have been able to borrow the Science Work Program from a neighbouring school and the textbooks should be here this week." A small prayer was silently muttered as I left the room and walked across the foyer to my empty and now somewhat lonely room. Miss Higgins had wondered off somewhere and was to be no help to me in the future. I obviously was not the man for her to snare into the security of marriage nor anything else for that matter!

The proffered literature from our friendly neighbouring school relived some of my stress. Teaching my own class I might probably be able to handle, but writing curriculum documents and all of the necessary instructions and activities for teaching an entire school was a matter for more experienced personages.

In handing over these documents, the Head had also comment equally casually "Oh, and by-the-way. I would like you to assist Mrs Hughes as the Male Physical Education teacher."

Another bombshell! My qualifications for this new job was the obvious fact that I was the youngest male teacher in the school. I would later find that this qualification would lead me into a variety of other interesting school appointments well outside of my qualifications and comfort zone. Still, the Teachers' College had anticipated just such promotion to HOD (Male Physical Education) and had rigorously trained us all in all manner of physical education pursuits, from the theoretic details of health and hygiene to the rigorous physical activities of football and ballroom dancing. At least I thought that I might be able to survive this new duty and actually be of some assistance. As it eventuated, Mrs Hughes was a modern dance specialist and I found that having two left feet in this branch of physical activity made me the idea 'comic relief' for this unholy partnership. Most of the boys thought that my clumsiness was for their self-esteem but the girls had a good idea of my artistic talent.

Back in the shelter of my laboratory/classroom with my new-found bounty and power, the old feelings of planned experimentation, which I had felt in my little backyard shack as a boy scientist, returned. Here I was with two state-of-the-art teaching laboratories, and extensive preparation room and the total freedom of ordering any piece of equipment I liked. My boyhood fantasies had finally come to fruition!

Miss Hermione Higgins had finally sauntered in with an attitude of bored disinterest and sat down at one of the front benches. I thrust out my hand in my usual enthusiastic style and received a very cold and limp few fingers in response. I muttered something about sharing the responsibility of getting this place organised rather than me being Grand High Poohbah (Science) and received an indifferent shrug in reply.

"I'm not very interested in those things," she said in an arrogant monotone. "I don't see teaching science here as much use, really," she continued in a lazy drawl. "Most of these creatures will just join the Public Service soon anyway."

Well, that seemed to be the general attitude of a person who was to become almost ghost-like in her relationship with me. She had expressed no ideas whatsoever as to how to set up a science department and showed little interest in doing any part of the huge amount of work which was now confronting me.

"Just give me the work program when its finished and I'll teach it," she vaguely promised and left the room.

We had very little personal contact after that and there was no social interaction whatsoever. She seemed to be one of those insular persons who did not want to make friends nor influence anyone. If she was happy within herself, I certainly saw no signs of it, and she did not seem to make any friends with the other women on the staff either. She would appear at nine in the morning and disappear after the last class at three in the afternoon. The exception was on the compulsory after-school staff meeting each month during which she would sit silently at the back of the room reading a magazine or looking out the window.

Coming back to the real world and feeling quite alone, I opened the Government book and ran my eye down the long list of equipment which I could buy – provided it exceeded three hundred pounds for each item. Now that was a lot of money in 1965! My father only got about twenty pounds per week and my first salary was going to be just a little over that! I looked at the list of items and on the tear-out order forms began to build my empire:

Balances: electronic – three, please. One for each laboratory and one for the Preparation Room.

Centrifuge: bench type – looks good but I wasn't sure where I would use it.

Chair: office, swivel – that would be comfortable in my staffroom.

Incubators: biological – one of these would be enough for my 'animal room' next door.

Microscope: research binocular – this would be nice!

Oven with hotplate – very nice for my staffroom at lunchtime.

Refrigerators/Freezer – yes, I'll have two! One for biological specimens and one for my new 'staffroom' which was a corner of the main preparation room.

Tape recorder: reel-to-reel with PA system – I was sure that I would use that somehow.

Telescope: five-inch Newtonian – this would be good for teaching astronomy if the fogs lifted at night and students did not succumb to the cold.

Television sets: black and white, large screens – two of those rare appliances, which were only seen in some of the wealthiest homes, would be nice also. One for each of my two laboratories. Stands included.

And so, my list of expensive items went on until my imagination became exhausted. I did not feel that I was being extravagant, after all I had come from a poor family where purchasing anything required the utmost thought and only those items deemed necessary had money saved up for them. However, this was not my family's money, but never-the-less I did not want to fill my precious space with anything that was not going to be useful.

The next catalogue was of more immediate importance because it contained the smaller and more practical items which would be used on a daily basis. Moreover, it came from the State stores which had a notorious reputation for being difficult to extract any item, no matter how much it was needed. This book was much thicker that the other because it contained all of those items found within schools and their specialised subject areas such as science laboratories. This took a little longer because I would not only have to remember what I had used over my school and College days, but also to anticipate what was going to be needed by two hundred eager students who would soon descend upon me.

There were the usual laboratory items such as glassware in the form of test-tubes, beakers, flasks, measuring cylinders, Petrie dishes, specimen jars, reagent bottles for chemicals and some of the more exotic glass items such as barometer tubes, Wulf bottles, pipettes and burettes just to mention a few. There was the hardware section detailing various stands, clamps, gauzes, tripods and a multitude of gas burners other than those invented by Herr Bunsen's assistant and the important detail that my school could only use those burners made for bottled LPG gas not the town gas which I had used in laboratories at school and College in Sydney.

The lists went on and I revelled buying things which I had never seen in my own school laboratories. There were geological specimens by the hundreds; rocks, minerals fossils, landscape models and charts to identify various types of soil, including our local red brown dust. There were biological supplies ranging from microscope slides, stains, bottled specimens and even live rats - 'dissection for the performance of'. I ordered everything which I had ever heard of in my studies with some of the most useful items such as test-tubes, flasks, beakers and the like being ordered in multiple boxes each of one hundred items. However, I declined on the live rats. Perhaps Miss Higgins would like to keep them? No? but what a horrible thought. Miss Hermione Higgins - the Rat Woman of West Capital High!

It had been an emotional day. I had trekked across a red brown desert and had an unexpected meeting with my superiors. I had been promoted out of all expectation but with no increase in time, salary nor assistance and I had exceeded my boyhood fantasy of soon to acquire the perfect 'chemistry set'. With the sun starting to set over the nation's capital, I left the school grounds and went in search of the bus stop for my return journey back to the centre of the city. Whether it was the stress or length of the day I was not too sure nor did I even bother to think about it, but I soon found myself walking down the path to the main building at Capital House.

Dinner had started so I found my table with my welcoming friends of the previous night, dropped my briefcase which was now full of official papers as well as my huge textbook and went to get my meal. This being Monday night, the main course was a hash made up of last night's roast.

"Tough luck!" said Will when I told the assembled table of my first day of official work and my sudden but unofficial promotion.

"Lucky bastard!" said Jacko who never liked any authority and seemed to be pleased that at least one local minion had achieved some form of reluctant independence.

Later, as I turned off the light in my dingy room and climbed into the creaky bed with its hard government issue mattress, my mind whizzed about thinking now of the realities of my first day. I had been thrown into the deep end of the vast sea of Education and floundered about the best I could. What would the future bring?

Chapter Six: Arrivals and Departures

Well, my first week had started on a very unexpected note. I had wrongly assumed when leaving my home town that I would enter into a well-established Palace of Learning under the tutorship of some old wise sage of Science Education known as the Head of Department (Science). The palace was here to be sure, but it was empty; including lacking my wise old sage. Instead I was it! Wise and a sage? No! I was the Acting HOD (Science) but without the extra salary, assisting staff nor time off for preparation. It was expected that I would 'hold the fort' until a real HOD (Science of course) would show up: perhaps next year or even the year after depending up what other 'clerical errors' would occur in Appointments branch of the Education Department back in Sydney.

The timeline for the establishment of West Capital High had been rather blurred in that very dim world of government bureaucracy. Things get lost in the world of paper-shuffling from desk to desk and from one department to the next. We were here and ready to go! Well, almost! I found out about the complexities of starting up a school when at the end of the week I had telephoned the local Department of Administrative Administration to enquire about the potential arrival time of the big equipment – that worth over three hundred pounds from the Government stores.

"Who are you? West Capital is not due to be finished until next year! Quoted the limp voice of the Mandarin at the other end of the phone. Apparently one arm of the Government had forgotten to tell the other who had been told by the Assistant to the Private Secretary of the Minister who ordered our current conception that we had, in fact arrived and now occupied the buildings.

"Ummm" said with a vague and bewildered tone was my only comment. Luckily, I was using The School Phone; that single line of communication between our little world and that of the bigger one outside. This hallowed piece of communication equipment sat on the Headmaster's secretary's desk and was guarded during school hours by that same vigilant lady. She had reluctantly given me permission to use the sacred device as it was on official business. It was opportune that the Headmaster had just emerged from his office and had seen the look of startled horror on my face.

"What's wrong, Mr Shipley? You look like you've just be transferred to Whoop Whoop!" he said with his usual beaming smile. The place he mentioned was the almost legendary country town so far away from anywhere that teachers sent there would have to consult maps penned by the early explorers just to locate it. A posting there was considered to be a death-knell for new teachers and the ultimate banishment for those older hands who had crossed someone in the Department of Education.

I held my shaking hand over the phone and said in a trembling voice. "He said that we don't exist! We shouldn't be here according to the regulations and no equipment is going to arrive."

With a smile, the Headmaster took the telephone and with his voice beaming down the line quietly and firmly told the poor public servant that we did exist and that he as Headmaster may have to speak to his superiors about such ignorance of this minion's facts. Moreover, there was a very polite suggestion from the Head as to where exactly this junior clerk should put these regulations and that if the said items did not arrive within the week, very nasty things would come down from his good personal friend, the Minister of Administrative Administration.

The Headmaster put down the phone which was immediately snatched up by his secretary and once more hidden below the counter. "Your items will be arriving within the week." He said with a benevolent beam sending shadows moving around the room. I felt sorry for anyone who would get on the wrong side of Big Barry McWhirter.

"Wait a minute, Mr Shipley!" he said going into his office and reaching for his own telephone, which as a mark of his superior position was sitting on top of his desk for all to see. "I'll phone Sydney and see how your other order is coming along."

I secretly wished him luck as I knew that the wheels of the Department back in Sydney moved around very slowly, especially when it came to dispensing anything, whether it were equipment, salaries and especially answers to enquiries. True to his remarkable style, Big Barry went straight to the most senior of the Department's officials who also was a personal friend. A man like Big Barry who was also a long-serving school principal had many friends in the Department of Education. He would also have many enemies and it was one of his talents that he knew the right people and could happily offend the others.

'Big Barry' was the title which staff had given him behind his back but with a certain amount of admiration and affection. His Deputy, John McIntyre, who later became a good friend, confided in me one day after too many beers, that in previous schools the Head was also called the 'Smiling Assassin' as he had a very disarming way of 'carpeting' those staff members who had done the wrong thing and were now to be force-transferred to a school at Whoop Whoop outside of the boundaries of civilization

The Headmaster put down the phone and beamed in my direction; luckily not quite a death smile of the assassin. "Your equipment should start to arrive late next week also, but be prepared for some delay in some items. You know what the Department is like."

I only had a neophyte's concept of the Department's transient operations but I was learning. I was more concerned that my stores would be coming on the National Capital Express and was therefore subject to predations by the likes of the Wild Bunch, Butch Cassidy and Ned Kelly and his gang of train robbers. What our famous Ned would do with five hundred test-tubes, only a nineteen-year-old with a fertile imagination could wonder. I was more concerned about the boxes of delicate and explosive chemicals which were also on order. I had had some experience with such chemicals and knew that the appropriate combinations would make ideal explosives that any robber would be happy to have.

By the Friday of the first week, the small staff at West Capital had got to know each other quite well and they generally seemed to be a happy lot – except for Miss

Hermione Higgins. We all had an optimistic view that we would start this new school in the best way possible. Certainly, Big Barry had a lot to do with this as he was very well organised, supportive and no problem was too big nor small to have his full attention. His Deputy, John McIntyre was also an able and friendly administrator. It was his task to sort out all of the trivial administration which made a school work; the timetable of subjects and lessons throughout the week; room allocations for staff; and the coordination of subject work programs which had been translated from the remote Department's syllabi which were the instructions about what was to be taught in general terms. I was delighted to find that the Science Syllabus, which had been thought up by some knowledgeable team of experienced teachers back in Sydney, was extremely detailed and clear in the topics which were to be taught. In those uncomplicated days, this was simply an ordered list of extensive notes with headings and sub-headings and sub-sub-headings of the content of knowledge which was to be imparted to our students. In addition, it came with a separate book called 'Notes to the Syllabus (Science)'. This was a further expansion at great length and for the lazy science teacher, this could be simply taught page by page as theory.

I had also been provided with several work programs from several of our neighbouring and established schools which had real HODs (Science) and knew how to translate the syllabus into actual teaching program incorporating practical activities, classroom exercises, a varied style of teaching methods and examinations to test the unwary. Curriculum development had not been on the agenda at Teachers' College but it was relatively easy to modify someone else's' work into a sequenced plan. Well at least for the next topic of the first two grades which were about to descend upon us. I would have a busy weekend getting this ready and my introductory lessons prepared.

The weekend passed without any major dramas. On Saturday evening, after our sumptuous dinner of tough steak and four veg – the usual Saturday night fare - Jacko and Will introduced me to the local hotel, appropriately called the 'Statesman's Rest'. It contained no visible statesmen and the only resting going on were elbows on the bar. The 'Rest', as it was known, as there were no statesmen within miles of the Capital according to local wags, was the most popular pub in town for the younger set of low-grade public servants, seconded personnel and other people who generally worked for a living. It was a great place for consuming beer at the fastest rate possible and to pick up any gossip about what parties were on later that night. The Capital generally shut down after the pubs closed at ten o'clock in the evening and it was the usual custom for the younger set to go seeking some additional activity at a party, either at one of the lower standard hostels such as Capital House or in some poor soul's private home. The art of party-going was to drink up, buy a bottle or two and head off on foot to the party before ten o'clock closing. Coming back on foot after the party would be problem as Canberra at night was a difficult place to navigate, even if one could walk a straight line, or circles for that matter. Jacko had a parasitic view about such events as social gatherings so he usually dispensed with the 'buy a bottle or two' and went anyway with the express plan to procure drinks at the venue. Being the life of the party, he usually succeeded and would often leave well-stocked both internally and externally. For the later purpose, he usually wore a large duffle coat which had big pockets.

Saturday night was not one of classroom preparation. Neither was early Sunday morning. The ceiling of my small room with its single lightbulb finally came into focus about ten o'clock when the sunlight was beaming in a painful way through my window. I felt as though my head had fallen off during the night and had been used as a football by the many demons of my dreams. Breakfast had long since passed and Sunday in the nation's capital was not noted in those days for its cafes and takeaways. My upheaving stomach would have to wait for the greasy cold-meat salad of lunch time.

Eventually after several copious mouthfuls of water from the bathroom sink, I began to get a feeling of urgency and forced myself to get the appropriate documents and notebooks from my briefcase and prepared my first introductory lessons. The Teaching Methods dodderer at College had suggested, on one of his rare appearances, that we keep a 'Teachers' Diary'. This would be a book in which we could write our lesson plans and keep notes of events which occurred in the classroom. Little detail had been given by this worthy as how this was to be done and who had drifted off into one of his fits of mumblings about the 'good old days' when all a teacher needed was a textbook to teach from and a stout cane to maintain discipline. I preferred to prepare a more sequenced plan and so ruled up my diary with a section for its lesson sequence on one side and supplementary notes on the other. It was a very simple affair as the Notes to the Syllabus which I had been given were already a detailed sequence of factual material and the prescribed and only textbook for my course was the 'bible' which had been produced by the consortium of University gurus in Sydney. They too, had the philosophy that all a good teacher needed was a good textbook – the thicker the better. To be honest, it and the Teachers' Guide which went with it, were excellent references for any new teacher. I could just imagine some of my older colleagues who still believed in the 'textbook and stick' philosophy starting each lesson with:

"Sit down, shut up and read and summarise pages 58 to 212!"

That was not the new philosophy of teaching and I would only resort to such tactics if I was forced to do so. So, I thought of how I would conduct my first classes. In such a new school with no precedents, I imagined that the first few lessons would be but a mere introduction to me, the new room and the wonderful world of science. Accordingly, I wrote down on the left-hand side of my diary a possible sequence and on the right some reference pages to the 'bible' with notes about behaviour and laboratory safety.

'Planks' Smyth my good friend from Woodworking and Metalworking had given me some good advice over coffee in the staffroom earlier that week. After all he had 'seen it all before' and every hard going was considered by him as 'extra training value':

"Start of hard. Well, for the first two weeks at least." He said. "Remember that you are not their friend and some of them may also see you as an enemy of their freedom. The boys may see you as a rival and the girls may see you as potential boyfriend. Regardless, both sides will want to try you out in their first encounters." He continued.

"Students are actually very tribal when they get together. You have to be accepted into the tribe to be a good teacher. Come in showing some strength but learn their ways. Don't be too friendly nor too aloof and above all, speak softly but don't carry a big stick. You will also need to have a good sense of humour as well. Too severe and you will become the butt of their jokes. Too cold and they will generally ignore you and give you a hard time whenever they can." These seem to be very wise words coming from a man who had had a lot of experience.

"Just remember that some of them will put you to the test at the start. So, don't take any nonsense. Put them down firmly but gently. They are a new bunch so you have a good advantage in that they have yet to develop their sense of tribal collaboration." He concluded.

This worried me a little. We had had a good grounding in child psychology and our practice teaching sessions had given a brief encounter with some of the handling of the variations in the teenage psyche, but that was for someone else's class where discipline had already been established. This was to be my first introduction to forty or so young teenagers in my own classroom with no-one standing behind me to assist if I needed help. Of course, there was always the Deputy Principal and the Mistress-in-charge of girls, but they might as well be on the Moon if things got rough in the classroom. My thoughts ran off into a school jungle of savages with teachers being the 'big game' of some hostile tribe. I tried to write down a workable script for my own protection which included a sequence for entering the room, getting students to quietly assume their seats, paying attention and generally doing as they were told, but would it work?

Bright and early on the Monday morning, I picked up my paper bag full of treats and said my farewells to my friends at the breakfast table. There were general looks of commiseration and expressed sentiments of good luck.

"You poor bastard!" Jacko said and hoped that he would see me that evening.

My trek to the bus stop, the usual uncomfortable ride and the further trek to the school did very little to quell my apprehension.

As I got nearer to the school, l I saw signs of much activity – unlike my first encounter with the school. There was now a line of cars coming into the large carpark which had quickly replaced the dunes of red brown dust. Parents and their offspring were getting bags and the usual paraphernalia of school children out of their cars and walking up the path to the side entrance of the school. I don't recall anyone using the grand double doors of the main entry, except when the visiting dignitaries came, but they never stayed very long and Big Barry would always find some reason to hustle them out after a short time.

I began to get a little pride and my apprehension of being captured by the tribe and eaten began to subside. Both parents and children seemed to be almost as concerned as I was. Putting on a brave front and trying to think of myself as an experienced professional, I held my head high and walked into the small crowd. "Good morning" here and "hello" there, I said as I purposely sought the sanctuary of the staffroom to sign on for my first day as a teacher. I realised that my very presence in my dark suit and almost dust-free shoes, my shiny new brief case and the huge 'bible' under my other arm gave me some credibility and demanded authority.

"Oooh! Here's one of the teachers!" I expected to hear from the open mouth of some pimply-faced neophyte but all I got was hurried smiles from a small number of harried mothers attempting to get their small child out of the car and into the school.

Having reached the security of the staffroom and the company of some of my colleagues, who had mostly seen it all before, I relaxed and helped myself to a well-needed coffee.

"General assembly in the hall at nine!" Came the quick announcement from Little John as he poked his head through the door for a brief moment. The 'hall' was what was called the 'Indoor Eating Area' on the school construction plan and it was to serve as an assembly hall, gymnasium, tuck shop and, when the weather got cold, as an indoor eating area. The real Assembly Hall was shown on the master plan as being a separate structure sited where other piles of red brown dirt still stood and its construction would be commenced the next year, or perhaps the year after.

"Well, here we go!" Graham Fowles, our burley Head of English and one of older members of staff, said as he led our little group of twenty or so teachers out from the safety of the staffroom and down the short corridor to the hall. Chairs had been arranged in several rows at one end and a small lectern with microphone had been placed in front of these. Chairs had also been placed around the inside wall of the hall for the benefit of those parents who had remained with their children after dropping them off. John McIntyre our Deputy and Miss Morgenstern, our

Mistress-in-charge of Girls were busy shepherding little groups of children and their parents to their various allocations: the parents to the chairs against the wall of the hall and the children to its centre in front of the rows of chairs and lectern. It was quite a noisy affair but people seemed to be cooperating and there was an orderliness about their movements. Perhaps this was because the new suburb of West Capital had become an "Armed Services' enclave with most of the newly-arrived public servants coming from the government's many offices associated with the nation's defence around the country with many of its personnel still serving in the Defence forces.

We trooped in and were guided to our allotted chairs by Bernie, our janitor, groundsman and general school factotum. Bernie always seem to be there when he was needed and always did everything with a permanent smile on his face. He was a simple man with absolutely no distasteful faults of character that I could observe. No task was too small nor too large for Bernie to take on and one could always rely on the job being done to the best of his ability. He was the type of person who would be part of the strong glue which would hold any school together.

The new Heads of Departments were ushered into the front row of seats with three seats in the centre reserved for our Administrative Team of Headmaster, his Deputy and Mistress-in-charge of Girls. To my surprise I was also allowed to sit in the front row but right at the end closest to the open doors of the outside wall of the hall. Miss Higgins sat behind me with the other lower minions.

In due course, the parents were all seated along the wall, our John McIntyre and Miss Morgenstern took their seats and the Head appeared out of nowhere which he had an unsettling habit of doing. The children were seated on the floor in a large, unsorted gaggle in the centre of the hall. Silence as the Head took his place at the lectern.

This scene looked very different to the previous assemblies I had witnessed as both a student and a student teacher. There was no general restlessness as students shuffled in their seats or poked their neighbour or did all of the other things which young teenagers did when they were forced to 'sit quietly' in a school assembly. Moreover, the students all looked well-kempt and eager to listen to what was going to be their first introduction to the Headmaster and his new school. It was obvious to me that a considerable amount of thought and hard work had gone on in the months leading up to this event. The most obvious fact was that all of the students, every boy and girl, was dressed neatly and correctly in their school uniforms. This was like something out of some Private School yearbook. The girls and boys all wore a sky-blue blazer with its red, white and blue school mountain-shaped badge on its pocket, white shirts and a blue and white striped tie completed the very attractive uniform. The boys wore light grey shorts and girls wore a light grey skirt which came to just above their knees. Miss Morgenstern had seen to that length in an age when the miniskirt was starting to creep its way up the legs of young girls. She would have 'inspection' every morning at First Assembly and personally check the lengths of these skirts. Heaven help any saucy lass who raised the hem by even the slightest amount. The students all had a light cream 'boater hat' with a band denoting the three stripes of the school's colours of red, white and blue. These hats had been politely removed and now rested in the laps of their owners. Not a scruffy urchin to be seen anywhere and all of the ties had been knotted correctly and were tucked into the blazer of their owners. Nothing like the rows of scruffy 'inmates' from my old practice teaching days.

"Welcome to West Capital High School." Was Barry McWhirter's first words in his new school, and his bright beam of a smile spread out through the large hall only now was only partly filled with our little group of pupils. We all sat and listened to what great words would come from our leader who now spoke in a good, firm voice which would probably have made the microphone redundant. He went on to give the background to the school's necessity in this new suburb and within a rapidly-developing city. This was a time of sudden expansion when whole Government departments were uprooted from the capital cities of the various states and moved here to the Capital. Construction of the school was ongoing and so we would all have to be mindful of the machinery, piles of material and the many workers who went about their purposeful activities not far from where we were sitting. As if by cue, a jackhammer started up just outside the hall.

"We only have two school guidelines here at West Capital." Big Barry went on. There was a pause whilst we all thought of how a school could run on just two school 'guidelines'. In another school, these would have been termed the 'school rules' and would have been laid down very much like the Ten Commandments of Moses. My own school, Madgewick had a list of rules which went over the page with the words 'don't' and 'punished' figuring prominently. The Head continued:

"My guidelines are simple and for the benefit of everyone." There was a slight mumbling of humour by us lesser minions seated behind him.

"Firstly, a school must be a happy place." This was something new to any set of school rules which I had ever seen. Mostly happy schools tended to come about despite the rules but by a rare combination of good staff-pupil-parent relationships. Unhappy schools came about due to the natural process of adult staff imposing strict rules on young children, especially those who had potentially criminal minds. I wondered whether or not my science colleague would have a happy class. Her life did not seem to have much of this quality in it.

"My second guideline" Big Barry continued: "is that no-one has the right to interfere with the education of others." He said this with only just the slightest turning of his head to the minions behind, with the suggestion that these rules, and especially the latter one applied to staff as well as to students.

"All behaviour and activity in this school will be centred around cooperation, respect for others and the need to try for one's own personal best. These two guidelines will ensure that we will all make this a school one of excellence."

By now we all had realised that Barry McWhirter was not a principal of the 'old school' but someone with an excellent vision for the future with a keen knowledge of the psychology of education. He went on to elaborate several of his other plans for the operation of the school. The student body, whilst still small, was to be divided into four co-educational groups or Houses to promote active but respectful rivalry. These were named after four local early explorers supported by the idealised mountain on the school badge with its motto "Outward and Upward". No vague Latin inscription here, but an exhortation for all to go out and explore and climb as high as they could in their personal life.

The worshipping of the elite student had no place in West Capital. The three pillars of the school were like the three peaks of the mountain on the school badge and were meant to be the academic, sporting and service lives of the students. Personal successes in any of these fields would score valuable points towards the three House trophies which would be given to the winning Houses at the end of the year. Individuals who achieved outstanding success in any field would be publicly congratulated and would have the satisfaction that their success went towards the benefit of their House and school.

Barry McWhirter was establishing a strong school culture. That is, the tangible and intangible things which clearly defined the nature of the school and how its people behaved towards each other and the general public at large. In time this was to become very clearly defined and students, parents and staff became proud of the standards which West Capital High achieved both academical, on the sporting field and in their behaviour to society in general. West Capital was going to be an exceptional school.

The Headmaster finished his short but inspiring speech and received wide acceptance and acclaim from the few parents who were present. His sentiments about respectful cooperation and the suggestion that the school was to be a collective partnership between students, parents and staff went down well. After a brief introduction to his staff, during which I felt rather exposed when it was my turn to stand and smile, the Headmaster handed over to his Deputy who then went through the detailed administration that was now necessary and the sorting out of students into their respective houses and classes. It was obvious that John McIntyre was an experienced administrator, for he had all of the students already arranged into Year and Class groups. No selective grading of classes here! The two small year groups were arranged into two classes each, initially of their own choice as many of the students had been together in our 'feeder' school which had been over-crowded and at some distance to the new suburb. Luckily there was very little problem here and with a little resorting, the numbers became almost equal in the two classes of each year.

Each of Year 7 and Year 8, the first two years of secondary school were sent to opposite ends of the hall under the supervision of their new Year Coordinators who were Miss Greenacre and Mr Withers respectively. The two-Year Coordinators then handed out the detailed timetable for each of the two classes which had been previously devised by the Deputy Principal. These timetables gave the students the scheduled lesson times for each of the days of the week. Each day had been broken up into six lessons with a short recess after the first two and a longer lunch period after the fourth lesson. These details and other minor ones such as the dress codes for physical education, a map of the operating classroom locations with the out-of-bounds areas. The functions of the School Canteen were also included in these short notes and some of the volunteer mothers already beamed from the servery which had suddenly opened at the end of the Headmaster's speech.

Having sorted out each of the two Year groups into classes as either Red or Blue, for there were to be no hint of grading here, the students were given a short recess and then told to report to their first class for Period Three, Monday.

Having also received these notes before the start of school, I found that my first class would be 2 Red in Laboratory 1, my teaching room. The short break gave me time to have a very quick cup of coffee with my excited colleagues in the staffroom and then to scurry across the vestibule to my domain and make things look like I was ready. It was hard to do in an empty laboratory which had ten large but empty rectangular benches and chairs for forty students.

There was no school bell, as it was expected that students and staff would learn to be responsible for their own movements and would learn to be on time for scheduled activities. Each classroom and other places of habitation had a clock and there also was a public address speaker in each room. This was used infrequently and initially only at the start of day in Period One after the classes had been settled and then only for brief announcements of any variation in the daily routine. This was usually done by Mrs. Adams, the Headmaster's very organised and motherly secretary. Shirley was another person in the school who always smiled and could handle any impossible situation as though it was a mere trifle. However, her office and that of the Headmaster were definitely out of bounds to everyone and woe betide any trespassers or attempted borrowing of stationery or equipment!

Five minutes to the start of class: my first class as a proper teacher. No Master Teacher behind the scenes, just me and about forty fourteen-year-olds. Soon two groups of eager-looking children began to assemble at both laboratory doors.

"Line up from here!" I said sternly, my legs slightly shaking and my face set in what I though was a mature visage of the experienced teacher. I was only five years their senior but I was often mistaken for someone several years my junior. Acting should have been a course at the Teachers' College because I felt like I needed a quick lesson in how to act the part of Mr Tom Shipley, Experienced Science Teacher.

To my surprise, the students quickly assembled themselves into two straight and parallel lines: girls closest to the wall and boys on the outside. They had probably been trained that way in their previous school so who was I to re-invent the wheel or in this case parallel lines!

"Make sure that you have all of your necessary gear out and leave your bags outside." I gave the usual much-practiced banter given by science teachers I had heard during Practice Teaching and hoped that my voice did not break mid-sentence. There would be no pilfering of science equipment in MY laboratory, even if it contained no equipment as yet. The girls went in first followed by the boys. I was struck by the orderliness of the group. Where was the pushing, poking, teasing and hurried conversation which I had observed during my student years? This looked like a good group.

Miss Higgins had finally appeared at her door of the other laboratory and had simply told the group to go inside and sit down. There was a little noise during this movement which was quietened by a low "shut-up" coming from inside.

In my laboratory I gave them the instruction that they should sit no more than five per bench and that initially they could sit with their friends as civilized students until proven otherwise. This was a superfluous statement as they had already seated themselves and were quietly waiting for my instruction. Taking out the Class Roll I had been given, and a blank seating plan which I had drawn up, I quickly called the roll and marked the number of the student, which was against their name in the roll, onto the seating plan. This would be permanent seating I intoned in a serious voice as well as I could muster, modelling it on that of an actor I had seen playing the role of a guard in a German prisoner-of-war movie. Variations could be made on application was my only dispensation to these potential public servants. In fact, such a plan would help me learn the student's names very quickly and also allow a quick check in marking the roll each lesson. All I had to do for this minor but important administrative bugbear was to look for vacant seats and then check who was missing. This worked most of the time except when members of a bench decided to play 'musical chairs'. I would have to learn who everyone was in a hurry.

My first lesson seemed to be successful. The class had entered the room relatively quietly and were attentive to my instructions which had been delivered in what I thought was a gruff, no-nonsense manner. The textbooks had been issued and there had been some free time to peruse their contents to marvel at the scope and breadth of the world of science. The size of the book seemed to suggest other attributes such as the vast knowledge which had been accumulated yet so far and I wondered whether or not the students had the thought of 'never mind the contents, feel the weight!'

Discipline, I was finding out was a matter of personal relationships between the students and the teachers. The 'old school' concept that a good class is a silent one did not fit into my style of teaching. Rather, I liked Big Barry's guideline that 'no one had the right to interfere with another's education'. In classroom practice, this meant that there should be no talking but attentive listening when someone else was talking. This was instilled in the classes from the very beginning and applied to everyone in the class. Of course, there were times when the teacher had priority and the students were expected to have the good sense in realising when it was time to talk and time to listen.

There would be no shouting over the hubbub here! When the class were in a state of verbal exchange, I would simply stand in front of the room, fold my arms and give them what I called the 'Jack Benny' look. This was modelled on the famous American comedian who would gain extra laughs in a situation with his upright stance, folded arms and a long sideways glance with wide eyes, eyebrows raised and a general look of tired exasperation. This usually quietened a class down and with some exaggeration gained a few good-humoured laughs at my apparent discomfort and incredulity. In a tougher school this would have achieved a few glares from the class and a continuation of the noise, so discipline techniques would have to vary from class to class. Usually quite patience won over screaming at everyone to shut up or at the last resort, quiet exclusion of the offenders from class by sitting them at a 'time-out' desk at the back of the classroom. For the persistent offender at the back of the room exclusion meant leaving the room to sit on the floor just outside the door – with more than enough work for them to get on with. Extreme offenders required some extra effort and support from a higher power but I don't recall this happening at West Capital.

Discipline also could be had by selective interaction with the main offenders. In my schooldays this meant sending the perpetrator out of the room and giving him at least two cuts of the cane; this was often me. Girls were sent to the Mistress-in-Charge for a severe tongue lashing. Both were temporary fixes as there were anti-social students who collected extra 'street cred' from their peers by getting punished as often as possible. In many cases, some selective focus of attention was all that was needed. This did not mean calling young offender an idiot or worse, but rather some more humane comment such as directing a class question to the offender – hopefully a simple one which they could answer correctly and thus be given some of the praise that they really wanted.

Sometimes, a little bit of dispensed authority could often make use of some of the offender's natural abilities as a dominant personality. This had to be done carefully. Making me a Laboratory Prefect for example, was probably a bad decision on my school's part, but it gave me some wonderful opportunities to experiment in professional surroundings.

My first attempt at this dispensation strategy also had mixed results. My Class 9 Red had a number of 'interesting' personalities that required some slight attention. One in particular had newly arrived and stood out as a potential trouble-maker in a school not noted for such problem children. Albert Brough was his name. although you would ask for trouble if you called him by his given name. 'Bert' was how he liked to be called and the rest of the class found that it was also expedient to call 'Tough Brough' by his preferred shortened name. Bert had just arrived from Melbourne as his father had suddenly been transferred to his department's new offices in the Capital; a common occurrence in these days of Government expansion. Such moves often disadvantaged the whole family, especially the children who were suddenly pulled away from their friends and local activities. The Capital was a city of totally bored and dissatisfied children – and many adults as well. Bert had been an Australia Rules football fanatic and followed one of the Australian Football Leagues major teams. This sporting code did not exist or if it did it could not compete with the local football code of Rugby League. Bert was unhappy and generally growled at everyone and hated everything else. He also had a physique which suited this hostility. He was short and stocky with rather a large head, a mass of black hair cut in the new 'Beatles' fashion and his eyebrows met together over two small, suspicious pig-like eyes. His mouth was always fixed into a permanent scowl. He was difficult to get on with in class until my second encounter when I quietly came up behind him in class just as he was about throw a large and sloppy wad of chewed paper at another student.

"So, you like AFL?" I surmised. This was a good guess as I knew that he came from Melbourne and if one did not like AFL there, then one's sanity was in serious doubt.

"Yeah. What of it?" came a low growl accompanied by a belligerent look.

"Who do you go for? I'm a fan of Carlton Club." I lied.

"Yeah?" said the astounded Bert who had thought that everyone in the Capital only followed the thugs of Rugby who wouldn't know a Behind from a Bump.

"I go for the Bombers," he replied with a look that suggested that there really was a young boy behind that hard face. "But the Blues aren't too bad." He conceded, putting his chewed missile under his desk and opening his book for the first time.

That little discussion had changed Bert's classroom behaviour; however, it reduced my intellectual standing with my colleagues somewhat, for Bert had decided that I was another poor soul who had been sent to this AFL-deprived penal colony. It thus became his duty to leave a copy of Melbourne's most well-known scandal sheet newspaper at the staff common room for my literary refreshment. As this newspaper always had interesting headlines of the most improbable and sensational nature, usually involving sex, violence and the depraved antics of AFL footballers or politicians, my colleagues suddenly began to wonder at this new turn in my literary preference. The paper also had a semi-clad Page Three Girl which did not help my credibility as a 'nice young man'.

There was another new recruit to Bert's class who seemed to rub him up the wrong way. This was a young boy who had recently arrived from Finland. His name was Aarno Gopnik and he seemed to be one of those people who were totally uncoordinated in everything they did. Talking almost constantly in a high-pitched voice was one aspect of his personality which he had yet to bring under control and I tried to assist with several gentle 'quieten down, Aarno!' in most lessons. One day during class, I received a note from the Headmaster's secretary to tell me that there was a telephone called in the office. This was probably yet another vague query about some of the equipment which I had ordered, but I thought that I should go. Normally I would not like to leave my class unattended but I thought that I could take a chance; they were all quietly working, except for Aarno who seemed as agitated as ever.

"Bert Brough!" I commanded. "I am making you Temporary Class Captain whilst I am out. You are responsible for any noise in the room." This I though at the time was a good idea as if anyone could control a class it would be 'Tough Brough'. A little more thought would have made me realise that this was like putting Ned Kelly and his gang in charge of bank security.

A big grin on the newly-appointed Poohbah's face as he sauntered out to the front of the room with added confidence and swagger:

"No problems, Sir" he said glaring around the room just looking for a victim.

I was only out of the room for a few minutes; the telephone call being only a simple and trivial manner. When I returned, the class was very and most unnaturally quiet. Too quiet! Some of the more reliable students had faint looks of apprehension which suggested to me that something was not quite right here. Bert sat confidently on the stool at my front bench with a very satisfied look on his face. Then it occurred to me: Aarno was no longer sitting at his place in the room.

"Where's Aarno?" I asked my Temporary Class Captain.

"Arrh, he gave me some lip Sir, an' I had to dis'plin him like." He replied.

There was a sudden chill down my spine as I wondered what cruel punishment 'Tough Brough' had inflicted on the feckless Fin.

Bert sauntered over to the bench cupboards under the window and slid open one of the larger doors. Inside, curled up in a very tight foetal position was the quivering and compressed Aarno.

"Umm. Well!" I limply said in mild rebuke, "This isn't Melbourne's Pentridge Prison here! We don't usually apply solitary confinement to our disruptive students." I continued as I hauled the rather shaken Aarno from his small cell. "Back to your seats and get on with your work." I commanded and then went to sit at my bench to recover my own nerves. I would have to be more selective in choosing class leaders in the future but luckily young

Bert left the school soon after the 'cupboard discipline' incident. Aarno managed to quieten down fearing that this new country had more unique cultural habits which would suddenly target its new arrivals.

On a general matter, I had never liked theoretical science. To me, science was an active method of personal exploration which demanded that the student find out new things by a series of serendipitous experiments and hands-on investigation. This had also been the philosophy of the College course which I had finished only a few months earlier, but it had yet to filter through to the Education Department in Sydney which still had the concept that a good textbook was worth copying. I did not see a classroom resembling a group of silent monks-scribes copying out huge tomes of work which was already a copy of someone else's copy. Unfortunately for the first week, with a bare laboratory, Miss Hermione Higgins and I had no choice in the matter: her with a standard lesson approach of 'open at page so-and-so, copy it out and do all of the exercises.' And me with a more casual approach of reading sections, discussing it and with a summary of the boring bits often with the aid of some funny diagram. The latter came from a mixture of a warped sense of humour and many years of my own school days in translating it to cartoons on the blackboard before my teacher arrived, mostly characures of these savants.

So, my teaching style had started its early days of haphazard development. I would accept no interruption but welcomed open enquiries and soon I found that the students accepted my view that the exploration of the world through science was a great adventure which I was on and that they could come with me. An innocent approach to be sure, but in this school with its motto and Big Barry's two school guidelines it worked. In a school with tougher students with an anti-intellectual attitude it may have been another story.

By the second week, large boxes had started to be delivered at the school's back Service Entrance in even larger trucks. They feel into two groups. The first group consisted of very large wooden crates of various shapes which seemed to arrive all at once and contained the 'over three hundred pounds' items from the Federal Government, having been sourced from local suppliers. The second group of boxes came in a long succession of smaller, cardboard boxes which came at all times of the day. This group came from 'Government Stores, Sydney' which was proudly stencilled on each box and contained all of the paraphernalia needed for a school laboratory. Sometimes a large cardboard box would be filled with items which had not been ordered but was in excess at Government Stores and so were sent out as a free item. One such box contained one hundred glass retorts; old fashioned round glass flasks with a very long glass spout. These had once been the delight of chemistry teachers who used them in vague experiments about distillation. They could also be seen portrayed in seventeenth century art works about alchemists and their mystical methods. These were of little use to my classes as we now possessed more modern distillation kits. It was suggested by some wag on the staff that these exotic glass containers would be useful as wine decanters and drinking devices much like Spanish wine-skins. So, the box was put aside for special staff occasions and never once did its contents get used for distillation. Looking at all of these cardboard boxes I had another vision of them being casually thrown one at a time on board the National Capital Express by failed members of the Cabbie Olympic team who now worked for the Department and then of the jumbled boxes' slow journey southward from Sydney. As Bushrangers and train robbers had little need for hundreds of test-tubes, specimen bottles and glass retorts, my precious cargo eventually arrived safely.

One of my students was Bennie, of my 8 Red class who was of very limited intelligence but very friendly and enthusiastic. Had Bennie been a Buddhist, he would probably have come back as a Labrador dog in his second life. He had that same open-mouth grin with a salivating tongue hanging out from one side. As he shared my enthusiasm for all of the large boxes which were now being rolled in by Bernie our janitor, I accepted his offer of help to open these treasures. So, it came to pass that one lunch hour I was busily opening the smaller boxes and checking off the invoices. Bennie had the job of carrying the opened and checked boxes into the preparation room when Jennie Greenacre came into the laboratory to ask if I wanted a lift that afternoon. She had kindly taken on the task of driving me and two of her female colleagues to the local shopping centre each afternoon; me to catch the bus home and the other two for daily coffee. It was just at that time that Bennie came back into the room dressed in my white laboratory coat, face mask and wearing a pair of bright blue rubber gloves which he held up much like a surgeon after scrubbing up.

"Don't touch me! I've been sterilized!" he said in a dramatic tone similar to that which he had heard on some television doctor program.

"Oh, how I wish!" said Jennie hurrying from the room to suppress her laughter. She also had Class 8 Red and had all but given up attempting to teach Bennie the beauty of French grammar. Bennie had difficulty with the grammar of English but adored his lovely French teacher and would sit dutifully in the first row admiring her with his head in his hands, mouth open and tongue dribbling saliva onto the desk. No Labrador could have shown any less adoration. This naturally gave Jennie the horrors. There would be days when she would burst into the staffroom with shudders and cries of "He's dribbling again!" and throw herself down at our long table which we all shared. Strong black coffee would soon be given as First Aid.

With most of our equipment stored away in what I thought would be logical places, I was confident now that real science lessons of the dramatic kind could now take place. Of course, this storage took considerable time and effort on my part as Miss Hermione Higgins had shown no signs of wanting to help. I was excited at opening all of these boxes as it reminded me of my meagre out-fitting of my small chemistry shed in the corner of our backyard at home, but only here it was on a gigantic scale. For the first few weeks I would stay back at school after classes and open boxes, tick off invoices and find some innovative place to store the new items. Jacko and Will grumbled at my lack of presence at the afternoon drinking sessions which had become standard between five and six thirty every day after work. I had devised a system of small, square labels for the larger cupboards which had both a stylised two-dimensional image of each item as well as its name. These went on the outside of the sliding doors in the cupboards in identical positions in each room. I was becoming a true acting head of science as schools were yet to hire Laboratory Assistants to do such laborious non-teaching tasks.

Armed with a large supply of chemicals and equipment of my own choosing, my science lessons started to become more interesting. Naturally they contained many demonstrations and many student experiments which were scheduled from the order in the textbook but there were also some additional activities which echoed my schoolboy past. Miss Hermione Higgins kept her practical activities to those few formal student experiments once a week which she had also performed and loathed in her own school days.

Teaching the topic of exothermic chemical reactions – those which gave off heat and light during the process – gave me an opportunity to introduce my students of Class 8 Red to the ancient Chinese invention of gunpowder. With forty eager teenage faces carefully watching my careful preparation at the front bench, I ground carbon blocks and sulfur sticks into separate piles of powders. Then with great and exaggerated caution, after having ordered the students to retreat a few desks away from the front bench, I powdered up lumps of potassium nitrate -

known as 'saltpetre' - I informed them – in the palm of my hand. I did this, I told them to eliminate the friction which would be caused by grinding it up like the other constituents in a standard mortar and pestle and which often caused explosions in gunpowder factories. This usually brough smiles of anticipation to the students.

"What if it went off in your hand?" asked some sadistic urchin from the back of the room. I had no answer to that but the thought was not a happy one.

The three powders were then carefully stirred together in a large glass beaker and poured onto a large sheet of paper. With great show and suitable explanation about the need to confine the powder, I rolled and wrapped the paper into a tight bundle. With my sorcerer's apprentices following at a respectful distance, I carried our explosive device through the corridor outside to the newly grassed area below the windows of my laboratory. With great care I laid the package down and punched a small hole into its top. Into this I placed a twist of nichrome wire which was connected to a long length of double electrical wire connected to a small telephone hand generator. Another flashback to my own schoolboy education.

"Stand back!" I commanded and the assembled conspirators did so hurriedly. I handed the generator to

Bennie and yelled "Fire in the Hole!"- the old miner's warning. Bennie stood there with his usual grin and mouth dripping saliva waiting to be told what to do.

"Turn the silly handle." I said in tired exasperation and he did so.

Instead of the optimistic predicted small explosion, there was instead a large sudden emission of smoke and a little flame. The dense cloud of grey smoke quickly rose up the wall of the building and into the open windows of the classrooms on the upper floor. Louds yells of protest and fear came back down from these same windows and the conspirators and their leader ran for it. Later at lunch, around the staffroom table there was an apology to all involved and to the Headmaster who sat at the end of the table. This incident afterwards became known as 'Shipley's Gunpowder Plot.'

Smoke seemed to play a major part in my lessons for some unknown reason. Not all of it was of my invention. One morning Class 8 Red was quietly working away on some boring textbook exercises and I sat behind the front bench feeling a little worse for wear having attended one of Jacko's 'cultural events' the night before. Sensing that something was not quite right – teachers develop this extra sense after a while – I looked up and counted the bodies hunched over their books writing. There were two bodies missing! They had come into the room and been marked present at the start of the class but now two had disappeared. Hurriedly and with some feeling of apprehension I walked up the central aisle of the room to the rear bench where the two bodies had been last seen. These belonged to two boys who were known to get up to mischief on rare occasions. Looking around and below the bench in case they had decided to perpetrate some crime on their fellow students below sight level, I saw nothing at all. Except!

There was a small trapdoor in the floorboards right at the very back of the room which was used by tradesmen to access some of the plumbing below the building. There was also an identical trapdoor in the adjoining laboratory belonging to Miss Hermione Higgins and both accessed the empty space below the laboratories. There was something suspicious about this particular trapdoor. Small tendrils of smoke where coming up from the cracks around its edges. Lifting up the brass recessed ring of the door, I suddenly heaved it open with all of my strength. With the rush of the opening trapdoor came a large volume of smoke which cleared to reveal four pimply-faced boys looking up wide-eyed and open mouthed, cigarettes dropping to the bare earth below. Expressions of apprehensive fear filled their faces. They knew that Big

Barry did not tolerate smoking in the school and it was one of the few crimes which would result in instant suspension or worse.

I stood up holding the trapdoor open and just laughed. What a sight! It was like four of the lesser imps of Hell had just been exposed to a more serene and holy world. The look on their faces was one of sheer terror at what dire consequences this representative of adult supremacy would inflict upon them.

"Get up out of there and bring your smokes with you!" I commanded. The four imps from Hell emerged to the laughter and ridicule of the rest of Class 8 Red. Closing the trapdoor, I seated my two missing bodies, Big Lazlo the Hungarian and Toby his acolyte, and then returned the other two to Miss Hermione Higgins next door who had Class 8 Blue busily copying out more pages and had not noticed the deficiency of students in her class.

Sometimes the students would get their own back. Classes and indeed whole schools are very tribal and it is the right of the younger members of any tribe to test the older members for any weakness they might have. One day it was my turn. I had Class 7 Blue, a good group of lively youngsters who as yet had not fully thrown off the innocence of Primary School and developed the rat-cunning of older teenagers. Or so I thought!

ANZAC Day was approaching; that time when the nation remembered the sacrifices of the Australian and New Zealand Army Corps (ANZACs) who first went to war together in 1914. War was still going on in Viet Nam and the suburb of West Capital was very much an armed forces enclave so such remembrances were considered to be important, especially in schools. One of the nicest girls in the class approached me whilst her colleagues were busy drawing a fossil specimen which I had given each bench. They all stopped and looked up at this approach. It probably resembled the scene from Dicken's 'Oliver twist' and she was going to ask for more. Perhaps.

Looking up at me with big innocent eyes, she handed me a rather complicated device all painted in a light blue colour. She told me that it had been made by her grandfather whilst he was a prisoner-of-war in Europe back in the 1940's. It consisted of a base consisting of a flat cylindrical tin made from an old tobacco tin surmounted by a series of small pipes which formed a framework of curved and straight tubes. In the centre of this complex network was a small paddlewheel. Emerging from this tubular maze was another long tube which appeared to have a small mouth-piece at its end.

She continued the story that her grandfather and his fellow prisoners would use this device to check on the health and weakness of their comrades. Each man would blow down the mouth piece and attempt to get the paddlewheel to rotate by the strength of their breath. Failure to move the paddlewheel would mean that the operator was weakening and should be given some extra portions of the cherished and limited food ration.

"Would I like to try it Sir?" she said with the pleading innocence that only a twelve-year-old could make. Back to 'Oliver twist'! By now the class had given up their drawings and were now intent in quietly watching the proceedings at the front of the room - subtle smiles of fiendish expectations on their faces.

"Why of course, Lucy." I replied, always ready to give any of my students some active encouragement. I was also gullible and an easy prey to such requests from the seemingly innocent.

I took the contraption and blew down the tube. Nothing happened. The paddlewheel stayed immoveable. Some of the class gave a light twitter of laughter at the failure of their teacher to move the paddlewheel.

Try harder, Sir!" someone said from the back of the room.

So, I tried harder. Only a slight movement in the paddlewheel and then it stopped. The laughter was now a little more universal and louder.

"Harder!" yelled an anonymous chorus.

I blew with all of my strength now and the paddlewheel began to turn. I returned the device to young Lucy with a beam of triumph. I was not the weakest of the tribe after all but by now the class was in hysterics of laughter. No doubt revelling in my success as a superior turner of paddlewheels.

"Sir, you should look in the mirror" said Phoebe, one of the more serious students in the front row. I turned and looked in the small mirror which I had attached to the front noticeboard so that I could watch the glass when my back was turned.

The reflection showed a rather shocked, pale-faced young man with a huge black moustache of soot streaked right across his face between mouth and nose. So that is where most of my hard-blown breath had gone! Up one of the many small blue tubes to a straight section having a row of holes primed with soot and which would be sited just beneath my nose. The more I blew, the more soot issued from these holes and painted the large, long black moustache which was really the cause of laughter from the class.

"You got me!" I meekly said with a grin that only partly showed through the soot and handed the device back to the proud Lucy who was now the superior being in Class 7 Blue. One needs to have a sense of humour to be a teacher and so I took no offence at being caught in such an innocent trap. In one respect it was a sign that I had been accepted by the class as being someone who was part of their tribe and could take a joke.

This acceptance was finally established and conferred upon me by the members of Class 8 Red during one sporting afternoon. As a special treat, the Headmaster had allowed the two classes of Year 8 to go to the local roller-skating rink at a nearby suburb during the usual Wednesday sports afternoon. It was only a short walk down the main spoke road to the rink in the neighbouring suburb. The venue was also being used by another, more established school who saw our small group as interlopers. Four members of our staff, including myself, joined the teachers of the other school in the small coffee shop attached to the rink. These teachers already had their heads buried in newspapers and did not want to known what was going on in the rink where a mass group of teenagers jostled for upright positions. My colleagues joined them in their ostrich-like activity but I joined our students in obtaining a set of roller skates. This was a fun activity and I had plenty of experience skating around the darkened streets back in my home suburb, considered to be a dangerous area, especially at night. I had learnt all of the tricks of skating from doing jumps over the many potholes in the road to getting a lift by hanging onto the back corners of slow trucks and vans which occasionally came down our street.

The rink was crowded with aggressive, jostling teenagers who saw an easy target when a young teacher made the mistake of stepping into the crowd. Interschool rivalry went by the board as the occasional 'accidental' push in the back occurred or an occasional leg was thrust out in front of me here and there. I knew the score and was ready for this game. A leg was suddenly thrust out of the teenage mass with the aim of tripping me over. No chance, I thought as I did a slight jump over the leg – much easier than a deep pothole – spun around and skated backwards away from the offending barrier.

"Ooooh!" said the mixed masses as I skated on.

Suddenly, the frustrated owner of the extended leg, an older tough from the other school, pushed one of our students over. A tussle broke out with groups of unstable, wheeled teenagers attempting to grab and shove their counterparts from the upright position.

The manager of the rink dashed in and pulled several of the offenders apart.

"Right! You lot from West Capital off the rink!" he yelled. I skated up to him and pointed out that the ring – or was it the rink – leader of the scuffle was from the other school and not from West Capital. When he got over the shock of seeing a teacher actually on skates, he reversed his decision and threw the other school off for a lengthy 'time out'. I resumed my innocent circle of skating, my hands behind my back and a feeling that justice had triumphed.

Big Lazlo, a competent skater who I had learned later had had the same training as I, sidled up to me.

"You're OK, Ships!" he said, using a nickname which the students had bestowed upon me. "You're one of us now." And he skated off into the anonymous crowd. I had been accepted as a member of the tribe and this story would ensure that I had great 'street cred' around the school. No one would be offensive to 'Ships the skater' from now on.

The year progressed happily for me. The Summer of the Arriving Boxes faded into the Autumn of Knowing my

Class and then into the freezing Winter of Despair known to all of those who lived in the nation's capital. West Capital was a new, show school and so was equipped with central heating which would keep every classroom and interior space warm and comfortable. A dual system of doors ensured that this warmth stayed in the building. There was only one problem. We had had a late autumn cold snap in this first year, with a heavy fall of snow and the temperature school interior dropped to only a few degrees to that of the outside which was well below freezing.

I found about the capital's winter when I awoke that morning in my little box of a room at Capital House. There was something strange about my hand when I eventually came into consciousness; curse Jacko and his extended social life! My hand was frozen to the wall! Having the window shut tight against the cold air of the night before, the condensation on the wall due to my breathing had cooled to below freezing and unfortunately my bare hand was attached to it. In sudden panic, I pulled my hand away from the glistening wall, leaving some hair and skin still embedded in the ice.

Finally, later that morning and wearing my best thermal underwear, a thin pullover over that, a thick white shirt, another pullover and my usual dark suit I had reached the assumed safety of my laboratory. The snow fell outside and the double-glazed windows were tightly closed. The temperature was still nudging freezing point when the students rushed in hoping to find some warmth compared to the open vestibule outside.

"It's cold, Sir!" someone cried. The boys of 7 Blue wore shorts and even the length of the girls skirts down to their knees as inspected by the Dragon Lady that morning did little to help. "Turn on the heating, please," pleaded another.

I looked at them with some degree of sorrow and considerable guilt and replied through my chattering teeth:

"It's not on!" I bleated. "they haven't come to turn on the master switch!" I continued.

The central heating, like everything in the Capital was regulated by Public Service Regulations. Big Barry had been on the telephone since he had arrived at the school with snow still on his coat shoulders and had gotten nowhere. The Department of Administrative Administration had haughtily explained that it was none of their affair as it was a Public Works matter. This was serious. Public Works were staffed by ex-tradies who always followed the rules for 'reasons of safety' they said. Winter started on the First of June in the Southern Hemisphere and it was only the Thirtieth of May so for safety reasons, the large gas tanks which provide fuel for the central heating were not going to be turned on. The Earth would freeze over first and, I honestly thought on that day, that the next Ice Age had indeed arrived.

Innovation and making do with equipment at hand has always been a trait of most teachers. The smaller gas tanks which provided gas for our laboratory Bunsen burners were not under the control of Public Works. This was yet another anomaly about how government worked in the Capital. Soon each of my laboratory benches had at least four Bunsen burners burning brightly with pathetic groups of shivering children trying to warm their hands – using the bright, luminous flame, of course.

We survived that cold day and within the week Public Works had deigned to arrive and turn on the gas. We were saved, although Graham Fowles, who was also in charge of History, was able to give a practical account of Napoleon's retreat from Moscow by having his hapless class trudge in an apparently endless line across the playground in the snow.

The school once more became warm and the end of the year approached. It was typical of schools to have people leaving the staff. As in the old Shakespearian play, the title of which I had forgotten, some achieve leaving, and others have leaving thrust upon them. Marge Dagworthy was one of the former, having met a suave member of the Peruvian Embassy and was resigning to go with her Rodrigo back to his home country where the people had a reputation for having good natures and a strong caring for family. Miss Hermione Higgins was of the latter type and her indifference and general lack of effort, even after many counselling sessions with the Headmaster, had been offered a transfer to Whoop Whoop which she could not refuse. Instead, she had resigned and left the school without any farewells and in the same vaporous manner in which she had arrived. We later found out that she had joined the Department of Administrative Administration as a Graduate Clerk (Base Grade) and would probably spend the rest of her career sending obnoxious letters to schools informing them that they did not really exist.

Chapter Seven: A Man of Experience

I had survived my first year of teaching mentally intact – well, almost. I had learned many valuable lessons about how students behaved, both individually and as a tribe and I had a comfortable feeling that I had been accepted as one of them. Perhaps this was because I still thought in terms of an older teenager. They were the younger versions of me. Perhaps it was because I had not put myself on a pedestal and delivered sermons from above with dire punishments for any lower minion who stepped out of line. I had tried to be fair as well as firm and had shown that I had a sense of humour and could take a joke as well as dish it out.

I had been very lucky to arrive in a school with good students and a Headmaster who was both a strong father figure to the students – and to some of the staff – as well as an administrator well ahead of his time. The school culture had been set up as one of mutual respect, cooperation and a strong belief in the school motto of 'Outward and Upward'. It was amazing how the students had taken to their fashionable school uniform and wore it with pride within the school and on the many local outings which the school undertook into the wider community. It was a bad weekend when the school was not open and students were there playing tennis or basketball on the newly-constructed courts or assisting with some project in the Woodworking/Metalworking block. If I came along on a weekend to set up some complex apparatus in the preparation room or change some of the displays, there were usually a few volunteers who wanted to help. It had truly become a community school.

On the first day of school in that second year, I wandered up the hill from Capital House to the bus stop, having survived the partly-cooked eggs from breakfast and waited the usual hour for my regular bus which came very irregularly. The route had expanded and now made a huge curve around the fringes of the outer western suburbs of the growing Capital. I watched out of my window as the bus ambled through more new streets, and houses now emitting a few of the newly arrived public servants who had been suddenly relocated from their homes in other cities of the Commonwealth.

There was still the long walk from my final stop to the school. No one in the Transport Section of the Department of Administrative Administration had thought to change the bus route out to this extremity. I had a horrible vision of Miss Hermione Higgins, now one of the powerful lower minions of this department stamping such a route change with a large red stamp which read 'NOT APPROVED!"

My final arrival at the school contrasted greatly with that of my first day almost exactly a year ago. No mounds of red brown dust here now! There was a well-planned bitumen car park backed by two new tennis courts with artificial green surfaces and beyond that two full-sized bitumen basketball courts. Extending off into the distance beyond these facilities were the extensive playing fields of newly-laid green grass.

There were new buildings too. The Department of Public Works had really worked hard once the due day for the building of the school had been settled. This was mainly due to the hard work of Big Barry McWhirter who had not only insisted that we did exist in those initial weeks but that the rest of the school should be finished poste haste. Big Barry obviously knew someone in high places, as there had been a fever pitch of building in the first year of the school's existence and over the school holidays at the end of the year. There had been only one small glitch in this construction frenzy. That was the day, early in my first year when I had come to the school one weekend and had borrowed some paint which I had found in the school maintenance store. I had then painted the glass backing of each of the two fume cupboards which connected each of the two laboratories to the preparation room. These fume cupboards or 'hoods' had glass fronts and backs which could be raised so that smelly chemical reactions could be performed within them. It also enabled one class to see through into the next and often there would be distractions as some urchin from one class would pull faces or make some obscene gesture to some offended party in the other laboratory. I thought that the easiest way to prevent this interchange of visual communication was to paint the backs of these glass cupboards with opaque white paint. Very satisfying, after all, it was in the blood as my father was a maintenance painter in the power station back home.

Bad idea! Suddenly I was confronted by a bull-headed person who had declared me black. I wasn't sure whether this was some racist slur or a failure in his eyesight but it meant that all of the workers downed tools and walked off the job to have yet another cup of tea in their tea room shed. The Australasian Painters' Union had objected to this mere teacher doing some of their work when he was not a fully paid up member of their union. I was, at that time, the school representative of our own Australasian Federation of Teachers but apparently the APU and the AFT adhered to different socialist perspectives so there was no compromise. So much for solidarity, brother!

It took considerable sweet talking and broad beaming of smile from Big Barry to explain to both the foreman from Public Works and the local official of the APU that I had meant no harm and I gave both personages a very genuine apology, including the fact that my father was also a card-carrying member of the APU in Sydney. This was all right then, and so work commenced.

With that black episode pushed out of my mind somewhere in the distant past, I walked into what now looked like a complete school. All four teaching blocks had been completed, although finishing touches were still being made to the latest two which now separated the 'indoor eating area' from the school playing fields. We still used that archaic term for the huge hall which was used for every 'indoor' mass activity such as physical education classes, school assemblies, school dances and the like and of course, for indoor eating during winter. It was somewhat like the Shakespearean play 'Macbeth' which is often only quietly called 'that Scottish play' for fear of bad luck. One did not refer to our hall as 'The Hall' in fear that Public Works would overhear this term and cancel plans for our real Hall which would be started in the next year – finances allowing and providing that no other project such as a politician's rest home was coming off the drawing board.

Public Works had finished the second block at the end of the previous year. This was parallel to the first and existing block, forming the extension of one side of the huge H which was the main plan. The two new blocks made up the second upright of the H and the 'indoor eating area' formed the cross-member between them and the next two blocks. This second block was a square court-yard affair like all of the others, but unlike the first block, which had the administration area, the entry vestibule and my two laboratories, it was open to the sky. Well, at least that would allow the smoke from some of the group experiments from science to get out more efficiently.

This block had two laboratories and a preparation room identical to that which I had outfitted and we had used for teaching in the previous year. It also had a small science department staff room and a Science Master's study. The latter was a small room which had an entry door at one end and small windows near the ceiling at the other. It looked like a miniature squash court and I and a few of my friends on the staff soon adopted it as the West Capital High Handball Court. Competitive matches were played there regularly at lunch time.

I had also decided to move out of my old laboratory and my 'staff room' which had been in the sunny 'animal room' of the preparation room. This was shared with an empty cage which should have contained live rats used for dissection. I had been trained in this zoological activity only in theory as the College also preferred not to keep live animals on site – the Drinking Set being the exception. There had also the theoretical explanation during one biology class on the humane method of killing these poor creatures prior to the dissection, but it was one aspect of the syllabus which I had so far avoided. I made do with using movies and transparencies on our new overhead projectors purchased from the Government for over three hundred pounds each.

I now had a real staffroom which contained four artificial-leather topped desks (Teachers for the use of). I had been the de facto Acting Head of Science in the past year but I did not presume to take over the new Subject Master's Study as I knew my place in the Education Department's hierarchy – right at the bottom, (Two-Year Trained Non-graduate) teachers.

On that first day of my second year, I found that the common room was uncommonly full of new members of staff. Our little band of about twenty had doubled in size and the student body was also about to do so in the forthcoming week. Promptly at nine, the Headmaster called his staff meeting to order and sat at the head of the table which was now completely occupied with the extra bodies standing around the walls of the room. Our pleasant lunch-time chats around this table would probably not be physically possible and so staff would have to retreat to their new subject staff rooms for their lunch break. Hopefully we would all assemble here for morning tea whether that be taken sitting or standing along the wall.

The Head gave one of his famous beaming smiles with his usual welcome to the school and introduced his Deputy John McIntyre who now took an official-looking piece of paper and said, almost in the same tones as the Headmaster a year ago:

"Now, let's see who we have here." He read of the list of names starting with the most senior staff beginning with Miss Morgenstern (the Dragon Lady) who had proven to be a good 'governess' to the girls and a very nice person below that hard and bulky exterior. Mr. Graham Fowles was still Head of English and ran the school Rugby teams and Mr. Withers as Head of Mathematics gave a depreciating smile and continued to keep to himself. Miss Jennie Greenacre, still Head of Languages and target of admiration of the older boys gave a sweet smile straight out of the French movie 'Gigi' and Mrs. Hughes as Head of Physical Education looked around the room with a 'who dares' glare. We all knew now that she could run a Marathon before breakfast. Finally, Mr Smyth as Head of Woodworking and Metalworking was the last of the previous years' Heads of Department and he gave everyone a confident wave which suggested that he had 'seen it all before'. There was no 'Uncle Tom Cobbly and all' as I had expected at the end of this long list but there was a new Head of Science! At this announcement I awoke up out of my bored examination of the coffee stains on the table and looked up to find this new apparition.

"I would like to welcome Mr. Bob Stanwell as HOD (Science) to West Capital High," Little John had just said. I followed his smile to a rather tall man standing against the wall at the back of the room. At first glance I saw that he wasn't my ideal as a mixture of Albert Einstein and Professor Lindenbrook from the Disney movie, but he had potential. He was thinner than Einstein but his hair was somewhat on par but less tasseled and it was fair, unlike that of the actor who played Lindenbrook. His returned shy smile suggested a friendly nature and it would be easy for him to meet any boy's stereotype of absent-minded scientist. It was no surprise many weeks later when Big Lazlo, who had been reluctantly promoted into Class 9 Red, had during a slip of the tongue, referred to Mr. Stanwell as "The Professor".

After the staff Meeting, we all retired to our new science staffroom for our own little meeting. The Professor came over as a friendly, good-natured type full of energy and was very thankful of my work in the school or 'holding the fort' as he called it. I had no qualms in relinquishing my previous position and was pleased to have a mentor and superior being to take the blame for science misdemeanours now that the school had suddenly doubled in size. My trust and admiration for the Professor soon developed when I realised with some joy, that here was an experienced teacher who, like myself, was also an eccentric and independent thinker. Heaven help any public servant or union boss who got on the bad side of the Professor! He was very soon a beloved and tolerated individual who became good friends with all, especially the Headmaster and myself.

The introduction to the Professor's personality and general outlook on life came when he took over my important role of carrying the newly arrived cardboard boxes, from the vestibule where they had been stacked, to the two preparation rooms. Bob had discovered something which I had overlooked in my dedicated adolescence: the internal set of double doors in the corridors leading to the new laboratories opened only in towards the vestibule. This meant that he would have to stop at each set of doors, put down his large stack of heavy boxes, open the doors and hold then in that position with one leg whilst picking up his cardboard load again. And so on to the next door. There were four sets of double doors designed to act as some sort of warm airlock during winter. They also had an automatic closing piston to close the doors when the body had passed through. This was too much for the Professor, so he arrived early at the school the next morning and, armed with a large screwdriver and other non-scientific tools, removed all of the internal doors. The next day, we found these doors lying on their side in the corridor. Big Barry heard the Professor's complaints and reasons for his actions and promptly asked Bernie, our hard-working and genial janitor to remove the bodies to a safe place where any Public Works inspector nor Union Representative of the APU would not find them. The basement with its winter gas tanks for the central heating would be the last place in the world they would look.

Back at our first science staff meeting, I looked around and found that I now also had two additional colleagues. I was introduced with considerable praise in having founded the science department and was doubly pleased when Bob commented that we would be using my well-developed teaching work program for that year until he had time for us to collectively develop a new one for the next. This was a good indication that my college training and my organisational ability had approached an acceptable standard rather than being a 'dog's breakfast' as I had feared.

My two new colleagues looked at me with some admiration and I, at twenty years of age felt like a 'old hand' who now could handle any classroom situation. They introduced themselves and gave a brief account of their experiences so far in this most variable and uncertain world of science teaching. Both men were university graduates and had had a diverse range of experience which would be useful in our developing school.

"Well," said the stocky fellow to my left who was obviously of Asian heritage "my name is Byron Lee and I teach biology." He said with a wide smile across a very broad face which had a remarkable similarity to statues of Hotei, the 'Laughing Budda' I had seen in tourist photos of Hong Kong. I felt that I would get to like this chap. He had gone on to state that his parents had given him the Chinese name of Lee Wang Wei but had accepted the more Anglicised name which he now preferred. He was third generation Australian; and his parents were well-to-do and lived in Sydney's affluent Eastern Suburbs.

Bob asked him how he had managed to get a country posting to the nation's capital and Byron gave us his sad story. He had been teaching Junior biology in a tough Secondary Modern School in London for several years but had returned home last December. He had promptly gone into the Department of Education and had asked for a job.

"We don't teach Junior Biology," the consulted lower minion in charge of Staff Appointments had haughtily replied, "we teach Integrated Science now." And continued stamping his documents with 'NOT APPROVED!' Byron had wandered out of the Department's 19th Century sandstone and attitude building in a state of shock and unemployment. It was over two weeks later, that his mother had thrown a cocktail party for friends and the most influential people of the city - one was no less than the Premier of the State. During the course of the evening and after too many tall glasses of the best Chardonnay, Byron had been introduced to this great man. Asked what he did for a living, Byron had bleated out that he was an unemployed Biology teacher who couldn't get a job because Junior Biology had been replaced by Integrated Science. Shocked at this confession and mindful of the great shortage of trained science teachers that had always existed in his State, the Premier had patted Byron on the shoulder and given him a friendly nod:

"Leave it to me, my friend. Where would you like to teach? You can start next week. Guaranteed! "

Byron had been overjoyed with this new prospect and woke up next morning somewhat bleary-eyed but looking forward with his new career, possibly in his local area.

Unfortunately, the Department works in inscrutable ways. The next morning, after also waking up bleary-eyed, The Premier had remembered his promise and when he finally showed up at his office later that afternoon dictated a message to his Private Secretary who sent it as an urgent memo to the Private Secretary to the Minister of Education. This worthy received the memo with some shock and dictated a more strongly-worded memo to his Private Secretary to be sent to the Private Secretary of the Director of Education, the most senior public servant and master of all things educational. This was received later that day with some considerable shock by the Director who then personally telephoned the Director of Staff Appointments who after several 'Yes, sirs' and 'certainly sir, I'll get right on it!' did so. With his telephone earpiece approaching meltdown, the Director now angrily telephoned the final minion in this unfortunate chain of events who had to suddenly stop his stamping of documents with 'NOT APPROVED!' and hurriedly note down all of the details of this Mr. Byron Lee's teaching qualifications and his request to be appointed to a school immediately as Science Teacher (Graduate Step three). When the air finally cleared and the minion had suitably recovered and after a needed short fit of stamping 'NOT 'APPROVED!' on several requests for staff to soothe his nerves, he wondered where this Mr Byron Lee should be sent. Somewhere evil and as far from the city as one could go. He immediately thought of Whoop Whoop High School, but that was already full and one of the few applications which always received the blue stamp of APPROVED! Looking at the list of recently-established schools, his eyes narrowed on 'West Capital'. He did not know where this school was, nor did he care but the name 'west' suggested somewhere way beyond the bounds of human settlement. That would do and so his blue stamp of approval would seal this Mr Byron Lee's fate once and for all.

Byron finished his story with a sad state of depreciation, possibly thinking that this purpose-driven error would make him appear substandard in our eyes. Far from it! We all thought that it was an excellent story, and so Byron was welcomed into the West Capital ranks with considerable pleasure. Biology had always been my weakest link so I immediately appreciated his new appointment to our little staff.

Byron's students soon found him an able and friendly teacher and because of his Asian heritage and stocky build affectionately called him 'Fuji'. Big Lazlo had spread the fictitious rumour that Mr. Lee was in fact related to the martial arts hero, Brue Lee so he was also called 'Bruce' behind his rather broad back. So it was that Byron had no problems with discipline, as the few toughs in the school thought that Fuji/Bruce was at least a Tenth Dan Black Belt in all of the martial arts and so was shown appropriate respect. Byron had never shown any interest in Asian martial arts but preferred chess instead. This was a well-guarded secret amongst the staff who would never depreciate the level of discipline of any colleague.

My other new colleague had sat and listened to Byron's story with an eager grin on his face. This was Jeremy Lockwood, Physicist. When it was his turn to divulge his life's story he did so with some relish and considerable enthusiasm accompanied with much waving of arms and general fits of excitement. He was indeed a real physicist, having come into teaching only recently and this was his first appointment. He had been working in one of the large hospitals in the western suburbs of Sydney in the Radiation Lab. It was his daily task to test the dosages of all of the dosimeters[7] which were handed in by the medicos who worked in any area which used dangerous isotopes in their daily treatments of patients with cancers. It was Jeremy's task to measure the dose of radiation received and monitor the health of the medicos and other workers and to prepare new dosimeters for the next day. He also had to prepare the same nuclear isotopes for preparation in their use in radiation therapy.

[7] Instruments which measure exposure to nuclear radiation.

This had become a rather limitless and boring routine for the restless Jeremy, so he had decided to find a job with less boring routine stress and become a teacher. Was he in for a shock! So, Jeremy had done the short three months bridging course for graduates which gave them some idea of how to instruct potentially-dangerous teenagers in the mystic arts of science. There was some sympathy for his outlook by all assembled, but this went over his head entirely and he continued in his excited manner to express his joy from escaping the threat and boredom of nuclear irradiation to the peace and quite of a high school classroom.

It soon became apparent that the new science department was going to be an interesting one in which to work, if we survived. The other teachers regarded our domain with some suspicion, thinking that with four such enthusiastic eccentrics running loose in the school could be trouble.

They were not wrong. I continued to follow my program of exciting demonstrations, having found that the Department had, by error, supplied us with more sodium metal than we had ordered. For the uninitiated, sodium metal is kept in oil-filled and tightly-sealed metal cans because it reacts with water, even that in the atmosphere, in a violent manner if in any size greater than a pea. Somewhere in the textbook's Teachers' Guide was the experiment in which a very small piece of sodium metal was to be reacted carefully and in very small amounts by placing it into a very wide and deep glass container filled to the top with water.

"Less than the size of a pea". Quoted the experimental instruction in the textbook's Teachers' Guide. This would produce a violent reaction with the 'less than pea' sized sodium expected to whizz around the surface of the water giving of considerable heat, flammable hydrogen gas and sometimes little flames. If Universal Indicator was added to the water beforehand, it would discolour it a green shade showing the neutral acidity of water. With the pea-sized pellet of sodium whizzing about on the surface of the water, this colour would change to a deep blue indicating that the rection was producing an alkaline sodium hydroxide solution as proposed. Too much sodium, the instruction warned would likely produce an unfortunate series of events culminating in an explosion.

So, in Period One of their first week and studying Acids and Bases, I set up a huge vat of water in front of Class 9 Red with a caution that this was a dangerous experiment. The first two rows, out of long-practiced habit, instinctively retreated behind their colleagues in the third row who now looked apprehensive as they were now to become the front line. I always followed appropriate safety guidelines. Despite the rumours which Class 9 Red had spread to the new incoming students about Ship's demonstrations, mostly as a way of denoting themselves as 'old hands' and scaring the younger ones, I had always put the students' safety as first priority. I knew the boundaries of such experiments; it was just that I felt that the teaching of science should show a little of the real excitement as well as the dangers of the discipline.

With the students at an expected state of excitement, I carefully extracted a block of oil-covered sodium metal and cut a small, pea-sized portion off one corner. I showed them the bright colour of the shiny, soft metal below its dull covering of oxide and used a pair of tweezers to drop it into the centre of the water's surface in the container.

"Ooooh!" said the class as the small piece of metal whizzed around the surface of the water in the glass container and the water changed predictably from green to blue. But there was no flame!

"Is that it?" protested Big Lazlo who was now standing behind the fattest boy in the class at the back of the room.

"Yes! Very disappointing!" I replied. The experiment had been performed as per the textbook and a teacher with little experience would have left it at that.

"Put some more in!" somebody cried from behind a wall of students, so I cut another piece of sodium off the oil-covered block. My concept of a pea was rather vague, not being a grower of vegetables and the green bullets at Capital House were no indications of size either. Instead, I cut off a large broad bean-sized piece of sodium and dropped it onto the water. With a loud 'bang!' it detonated as the larger mass of sodium reacted even more violently with the water producing large amounts of heat and flammable hydrogen gas. Smoke once more filled the room as did cries of terror and shock from the students in the third row.

The room and its occupants were still intact. No one had been showered with the small pieces of burning sodium metal which now formed miniature spot fires on my desk. My nice almost-white laboratory coat had acquired a few more holes in it but the students were safe. One of the boys jumped up onto his desk and started to fan the air with his notebook to help clear it of smoke. Many of the other boys also joined up with their books in their hands.

"Don't worry, Sir. We'll take the blame!" someone said and I knew that they really appreciated my experiments.

Locky, as the students called Jeremy Lockwood, was not as lucky as was I. He was an experienced physicist but much of his high school and undergraduate basic chemistry had been forgotten. He was now into the section of the work program dealing with exothermic and endothermic reactions[8]. He had also heard from his Class 9 Blue about the Mr, Shipley's 'Gunpowder Plot' of the previous year but had decided against doing such a dangerous experiment. Instead, on reading up from some old obscure chemistry book he had found in an equally old obscure bookshop, he had discovered a demonstration called 'the thermite reaction'. This seemed like a very exciting demonstration and so he prepared it for his class that day.

Bob, Byron and I had a spare period at that time and were sitting in our staffroom next door to Jeremy's lab to have yet another morning dose of coffee. Suddenly there were huge screams of terror coming from the laboratory next door. We put down our cups and ran out of the staffroom and into the courtyard. Locky's laboratory door flew open and a huge cloud of dense black smoke rolled out and flowed lazily across the floor. From it emerged a tall figure, black of faced and with small smoky tendrils coming from his hair. The remains of a long, wax taper, now extinguished, still tightly clutched in his hand.

---

[8] Chemical reactions which gave off (exothermic) or took in (endothermic) heat energy.

"Wow!" it said with excited enthusiasm "Was that a great experiment or what!"

We rushed into the laboratory whilst the blacken Jeremy wandered around the courtyard patting out the small fires in his hair. Inside was total chaos. The entire cohort of thirty-eight Class 9 Red students were now cowering in the back row of the laboratory, mostly under the laboratory benches. The teacher's demonstration desk now had a large blacked hole in its centres with an artistic circle of tall flames around its edges. The white insulation tiles of the ceiling above the bench were blackened also except where little patches flaked off and fell like some weird indoor snow fall. Bob used the small fire extinguisher which usually was clamped dusty and unwanted on the front wall to extinguish the flames on the bench and found that the black hole had also extended through its shelves below, through the floor boards and to the bare ground below were a malevolent molten red eye of the remains of Jeremey's experiment still glowed. Byron, seeing that the situation was under control – well almost – went out in search of the black-face figure who was last seen staggering around the courtyard leaving wisps of black smoke behind in his wake. Jeremy had put out his own person flames and now had sat down on the ground, finally letting go of the wax taper. Assured that his class was no longer in danger – now that their sorcerer having departed – Jeremy allowed Byron to take him to the staff room where his hair was patted down with a wet towel and his face generally restored to its excitable pink condition. Luckily there had been no injuries other than to the front bench, the ceiling above and the floor below.

Bob had quietened the class down in his usual fatherly style and Jeremy had returned to the laboratory to uncertain cheers and applause. Afterwards, Jeremy had described just how his experiment had gone astray. Consulting his old obscure chemistry book, which had come from the equally old obscure bookshop, he had read of this great thermite reaction very much exothermic and which produced temperatures which exceeded that of molten iron. However, no quantities had been given as this old obscure chemistry book was one of pure theory only as it had been written at a time when chemistry was taught by the book being copied out by suitably cowed and quietened students.

Jeremy had come to his own conclusions and had filled a stainless-steel beaker about the size of a small coffee cup with the dangerous thermite mixture (details withheld to protect the innocent). He had sat this beaker on a thin metal tray on the front bench and had set it off with a length of magnesium ribbon, itself a source of bright light and flame when lit using a lighted long wax taper. The resultant reaction gave a broad and very high flame of immense heat which reached up and scorched the ceiling. The stainless-steel beaker had completely melted with the intense heat and had burnt its way down through the thin metal tray, the thickness of the front bench and its shelves below and then through the floorboards to ground below the laboratory. This had been our resident nuclear physicist's version of a 'China Syndrome' in which a meltdown at a nuclear plant would cause the extreme hot nuclear metallic fuel to melt its way (theoretically) through the Earth to China.

Later, in the privacy of our own staffroom, Bob had suggested fairly firmly to us all that it was time that we should all keep our heads down - for a while at least. The Headmaster had listened to Bob's explanation of our latest exploits in science, after the indignant members of the local Fire Brigade had left, and had been reasonably tolerant but he had made it quite clear that he wanted good students not dead ones. This advice we all took most sincerely and with some regret, Jeremy announced that teaching science was really a very dangerous occupation and that he would be leaving at the end of term and returning to the safety of his radioactive isotopes. We were all saddened to hear this, because with some additional help in his demonstration techniques, Jeremy had the potential for being a very fine teacher.

After his sad departure, it was decided by Bob that we would now remember Jeremy's enthusiasm by holding an Annual Jeremy Lockwood Memorial Experiment. This would be a repeat of the thermite reaction to all Year 9 classes but using only such amount of the mixture which would just cover a small bottle cap. Even then, the flame would reach respectable heights. This remembrance activity however, would be postponed to the first anniversary of the original experiment, many months and into a new school. In the meantime, we were all to keep a low profile and keep our experiments within our own classroom and to follow the textbook's Teachers Guide to each boring letter.

This began a period of relative peace and quiet. Some of the other members of staff became unsettled, especially those who had classrooms near our four laboratories. What were the science staff plotting now? What were they really doing in those laboratories?

The students had settled down to normal laboratory experiments, some which were exciting on the small scale and others which were not. Nothing very exciting happened until one eventful morning, just after the start of Period One:

"Sir, come quick, Fuji's been killed!" the horror-struck student from 9 Blue screamed as she burst into the science staff room without knocking. We dashed out and along the corridor to Byron Lee's laboratory.

There on the floor was Byron, completely stretched out. A group of concerned students hovered over the body like excited vultures; the boys mostly with looks of horror on their faces and girls in tears standing a little way from the body. There was a small trickle of blood coming from behind Byron's head. Bod reached him first and raised his head which had turned to a faded white colour. A low moan came from his lips.

"He's OK! Go to your places and sit down and get on with your work." He commanded. The class slowly did as they were told but all had heads turned towards the inert body in the front of the room. Looks of apprehension and sorrow on their young faces.

Bob had managed to get Byron up to a sitting position and I applied a wet towel to his head and Jeremy was ready with some sterile gauze which he had taken from the laboratory's First Aid Box. Having recovered to some degree of consciousness, we lifted Byron up under each of his arms and slowly walked him back to the staff room. Bob rang for Miss Morgenstern, who was not only the school's Dragon Lady but also its First Aid Officer. She was there in double quick time and gave Byron's head a thorough examination and a stern demand to know what had happened.

Byron was conscious enough to mutter his sad story about how his reported 'death' had come about. This was no deliberate scientific experiment for a change, but an innocently received injury due to accidental causes. Bryon explained that he had just gotten his class settled in their seats and had launched into a detailed explanation of the sex-life of the warty newt when the loud speaker above his head suddenly crackled into life. Every room had one of these speakers hanging on the wall just above the centre of the blackboard. Occasionally, or much too frequently some said, Mrs. Adams, the School Secretary would come onto the Public Address system and make some announcement. Usually it was about some variation to school routine or an important decision of the Headmaster.

Byron had never liked any interruption to his lessons, being basically a very thorough and intense teacher. He was just about to explain the important and exciting facts about the sex life of the warty newt when the announcement suddenly issued loudly from above. Grasping the metre ruler which was on the sill of the blackboard, he had reached up to his maximum stretch and had given the offending loudspeaker and source of his interruption a defiant token whack. To his shock, Public Works had merely suspended these speakers onto a hook in the wall as a cost-saving measure. Consequently, the injured speaker, housed in a sizeable stout wooden box, came crashing down and hit Byron squarely in the centre of his upturned forehead and felled him to the ground. Surely there was a martial arts defence against such a sudden strike, thought some of the less-sensitive students after they had recovered from the lessons most recent science demonstration.

Later that morning, Byron returned to his other classes with a large strip of plaster across his small wound. Students who had yet to hear of Fuji's battle with the box naturally thought that he had been wound in some hand-to-hand combat against a large group of thugs who obviously would have all come away with many more severe injuries. For a short time at least, Byron's street cred hit new heights until the very efficient and extensive student grapevine passed on the real cause of his injuries. Shirley Adams, our tough but motherly School Secretary was most upset when she heard the story and hurried over to Byron's laboratory to express her sadness at being in some way the cause in his accident and the next day brought him one of her famous chocolate cakes which always appeared at the end of Term morning tea. Life in the science department eventually returned to normal.

The end of the term came and Jeremy was given a cheerful send off with the promise that he was not to try anything similar at the Nuclear Radiation Department of the local hospital. They had gratefully accepted his application for employment but we were in a time of nuclear uncertainty between the Soviet Union and America, so a home-grown nuclear event of similar proportions to the famous thermite reaction was to be avoided at all costs.

The short school holiday came and went very quickly and I returned to West Capital to find another new member of staff standing around alone in the common room. He introduced himself as Doug Flowers, a new member of the science staff.

"Poor bastard!" I replied "Are you insured?" I calmed his fears down by introducing myself as one of his science colleagues who had survived so far. He realised, perhaps, that my comments were in jest and so relaxed - for the moment. 'Dougy' as he was known by both staff and students alike, was one of those enthusiastic but inept characters who could have easily fallen into Jeremy Lockwood's place and reproduced his own original thermite experiment had Bob not cautioned him, somewhat hypocritically, about the needs for strict safety and about following any experimental method to the rules and to the gram. Dougy's initiation to our order of science eccentrics came on one fateful night.

Dougy was a young teacher with natural, although somewhat dopey good looks who soon became the swoon favourite of the older girls. His Class 7 Blue had a particularly large following and he would often be seen during playground duty walking slowly across the yard with a comet's tail of Year 7's following. His particular love was Astronomy and so it was not unusual nor was there any great feeling of apprehension by the school staff when Dougy announced that he would run an Astronomy Night Spectacular (his words). The Head and the professor thought that this would also be a good community activity, so with Doug's consent it was advertised as such in the school bulletin and over the loud speakers which had now been bolted to the wall by our very thorough janitor, Bernie. Everyone in the school community was invited. It was late autumn and whilst the weather was cold, it was the best time for sky observation, provided that it did not rain or the famous fogs of the region descend upon us.

Dougy had organised this activity down to every fine detail and had borrowed two other telescopes to add to ours. Each of the three telescopes was a standard Government-over-three-hundred-pound 5-inch reflecting Newtonian telescope mounted on a sturdy wooden tripod.

Dougy had asked Fuji and I to assist with two of the telescopes and he had consulted the relevant star charts and found that Monday in two weeks would be a good time to have the event. He had prepared worksheets for each of our three Years with questions about the Moon, the star Alpha Centauri and the planet Mars as all would be in good positions for observations. All students were given invitations and permission slips to take home to their parents and it was all set.

Surprisingly, on that night the weather was absolutely perfect and the sky was totally clear. The Moon was just coming up in its Last Quarter, Alpha Centauri shone brightly as one of the two Pointers of the Southern Cross and the planet Mars gave a strong, steady red glare overhead. Perfect!

All was going well. True to form, most of the students began to arrive punctually just after sunset with their parents. The Professor, our efficient Head of Department mustered them into the 'indoor eating area' and gave them a short welcome and the plan for the night's activities. The Headmaster beamed from the far wall where most of the staff were standing ready to join in the science department's apparent benign activity. Dougy had arranged the three telescopes at well-spaced places on a new, grass playing field and Fuji and I took up our positions at our allotted telescopes armed with a flashlight and heads full of interesting facts about our nominated celestial object. Soon groups of students, their parents and guests and interested members of staff arrived at each telescope and formed orderly lines of eager chatting silhouettes in the darkening gloom. All was going well.

Unfortunately, Dougy's detailed plan had left out one little technical detail. He was not aware of this problem but we had all assumed that he was and had provided a contingency plan against it.

Now the playing fields were serviced by an extensive and complex industrial-sized very high-pressure watering system. Right on their scheduled time, large tubes began rising out of the ground from their subterranean shelters and immense volumes of water at very high pressure began to rotate in thick circular scythes knocking down everything standing on the grass playing fields. These included students, parents, guests and teachers trying to hold onto their telescopes, flashlights and notes. Everyone took off and ran in all directions but mostly to the comforting lights of the dry school buildings at some distance from the biblical-grade deluge.

"Get the telescopes!" yelled Dougy.

"What's going on?" Fuji yelled, having been knocked over onto his back by a very high-pressure jet of water.

"Run for it!" I yelled with a sick feeling of stating the obvious.

"Head for the hall!" yelled the Professor in the midst of the chaos.

"Everyone to the Ark!" Noah would have yelled at a time like this.

Dougy just stood there with a sheaf of wet papers in his hand looking to the sky in silent prayer: "Why me? Lord!"

And so, we all ran for shelter of the school buildings soaking wet. This was to be an astronomy night to be remembered and not repeated! The Headmaster again expressed his desire that this would be the last of the Science Department's major activities for that year at least.

His wish was granted and the Science Department kept a lower subterranean-like profile for a while. Well, that's if you didn't count Fuji's Great Bat Scare which happened at the start of the new spring season. It had come about by some child's bringing in a 'dead bat' to Fuji's Year 7 Blue class. Or so she thought! Fuji put the little black body into an empty cardboard chalk box and shoved it under his front bench for later reference, his lesson at the time being more adventures of the warty newt; his favourite topic. A few weeks later, a very strong smell came from this very area, and Fuji realised that it was due to this harmless-looking chalk box. He was again teaching his Class 7 Blue at the time, a very nice group of our youngest boys and girls and it was they who alerted Fuji to the smell.

Fuji reached under the bench, extracted the old cardboard chalk box and removed its top. The 'dead bat' was alive! It had been only in a state of suspended animation for the cold of the winter. Now, inside a nice warm classroom it clawed its way over the edge of the box like some small black demon.

"It's alive!" yelled some boy from the front row who had seen too many old Frankenstein movies. With that, the bat took flight and flapped its way haphazardly around the classroom. Pandemonium ensured with students jumping up and also shrieking their way around the classroom but at a much lower level than the flight path of the poor bat.

"It'll get into my hair!" shrieked a chorus of terrified girls.

"Kill it!" shouted a group of blood-thirsty boys who had also seen too many Frankenstein movies.

"Sit down!" yelled Fuji with little effect.

Finally, the poor bat found its way through the door and into the courtyard just as the Professor was coming in to see what all of the noise was about. He had to duck quickly as the leather-winged creature flew over his head and to freedom.

"What the devil!" shouted the Professor.

Safe from any real entanglement and with blood lust now quelled, the students finally stopped yelling and looked at this white-coated newcomer wide-eyed and breathing heavily. With the Professor's entrance and the bat's exit, the students quickly resumed their seats: the girls with their hair completely in tangles as they had fought to keep their airborne marauder from getting into it; and the boys now fully recovered from their blood lust panting and wild-eyed. Fuji was now able to retake control of his class and silently vowed never to take in 'dead' specimens from volunteer collectors. From now on, all specimens would have to be in bottles. Science would also now definitely have to keep itself bottled up and keep on a low shelf.

They say that in a perfect world that all good things must come to an end. I had enjoyed my two years of 'Country Service' in West Capital. I could have been sent to a far distant high school such as Whoop Whoop simply by the bad luck of the pen at Appointments Branch in Sydney! Now it was time for me to move on.

As a Probationary Teacher (Non-graduate), I had been thoroughly inspected and given the 'Third Degree' (whatever that is!) by Inspectors from the Department's inquisition section in each of my two years. They in turn had sat in upon most of my lessons, examined all of my student's notebooks, poked into every nook and cranny of the laboratory and had long private sessions with Big Barry and the Professor. Their observations of my nervous, thoroughly planned, scripted and textbook Teachers' Guide experiments along with some kind words from my superiors, assured my promotion to the status of a full Teacher (Non-graduate) and the eventual issuing of my coveted Teachers' Certificate.

However, both of the worthy Inquisitors had given me a stern caution that I would not have much of a teaching career unless I acquired a university degree. I had never thought about this, as I did not consider myself as 'university material'. No one in my extended family nor friends had ever been to a university unless it was to carry out minor maintenance. Besides, how could I go to university and stay as a teacher? The answer, of course was to do the degree part-time. Unfortunately, the local university only offered two First Year courses towards a part-time Science degree: mathematics and psychology. The former I hated with a passion but the later looked mindful and interesting. I would have to reluctantly return home to Sydney where only one university offered a part-time science degree with a minimum period of study of seven years.

With some guilt and very much reluctance, I had handed in my Transfer papers to Big Barry who accepted them with some understanding and kindness and forwarded them off to Head Office where I hoped that some minion would stamp it with the blue stamp of approval.

I was beginning to have mixed feelings now. It was September and I had just celebrated my twenty-first birthday, so in the eyes of law I had finally shaken off my childhood and had finally became a man of good social standing. There had been a small celebration at the school in the common room on that last lunch hour with all of my friends at the school present and Miss Morgenstern and her girls in the Home Economics kitchen had baked me a cake. That evening, back at Capital House, Jacko and Will and some of my other cronies took me to the Statesman's Rest where at last I was able to finally have a drink legally.

My two years at West Capital had been a great introduction to teaching and I had learnt some valuable lessons about the relationships between teachers and students as well as between teachers and the Education Department. I had found that, with some initial firm acting on my part, I was able to fall into a comfortable relationship with most of the students in my classes. There had been some interesting characters, like Big Lazlo who had become one of my friends once I had been accepted into the tribe, and some more challenging students like Bert 'Tough' Brough who was never going to advance his education much past Year Nine because of his belligerent nature. Lazlo would do well because he was flexible; he had all of the personal charm and distortion of the truth that were desirable characteristics in politics, but poor Bert would probably end up running a crime syndicate back in his beloved Melbourne, no doubt contributing to bodies found in cupboards there.

My transfer came through near the end of the year and everyone at the school was disappointed that I was going, especially The Professor, Fuji and Dougy who had become my very good friends as well as fellow conspirators. We had all had a lot of adventures together in the many dubious but demonstrative science experiments and perilous student expeditions officially called 'school excursions'.

Class Nine Red were sad to see me go as they had looked forward to having me again next year: another one of the Head's advanced educational philosophies being that once a teacher had established a good bond with a class, he or she should carry them right through to the end of their Junior years. On my last day, I walked into their thoroughly-planned and unexpected surprise party. Everyone had brought along something. The girls who did Home Economics had baked and decorated yet another large cake of strange texture and doughy taste which read 'Goodbye Ships' in blue lettering. Others had brought along various biscuits, crisps and other assorted delicacies which had been hidden in their bags outside of the laboratory. They had managed to get into the laboratory early, no doubt with the help of The Professor or Bernie the janitor who would have trusted them to do the 'right thing', and had decorated it with streamers and balloons. A cartoon character of me had been drawn on the blackboard which reminded me of my early art career at Madgewick. The boys had found a large glass pneumatic trough in the Preparation Room, cleaned it thoroughly and were now adding bottles of lemonade, dry ginger ale and fruit juice to make up some concoction they called 'punch'. I quickly looked into the preparation room to check if the large drum of ethyl alcohol which was used in cleaning had not been tampered with. Everything being normal in the alcohol department, I brought out the hidden box of glass retorts and, after a quick demonstration in their newly-found use, handed them around as drinking containers. The students thought this very scientific and so the punch went down much better than it tasted.

Bennie, the alternative Labrador, had brought along two huge water melons, no doubt provided by his father who had a chain of fruit shops around the city. His father, I had found at our first meeting at last year's Parent-Teacher Night, was an adult version of his son, except that he had mastered his lower jaw so that it did not dribble saliva. Well, not too much except when he got excited and lapsed into voluble hand-waving Italian about the joys of good fruit and vegetables. Both may be classified as 'simple' by foolish teachers who relied completely on vague IQ scores, but both knew fruit and vegetables like no one else in the city. Bennie had already notched up several years of experience going to the markets out in the city's hidden and orphaned industrial area every morning at sunrise to pick the best of the imported crops. I had no doubt that Bennie would one day take over his father's lucrative empire and have more money than most of his classmates put together.

Dissection boards were produced, scrubbed down and a big knife was produced by the girls from Home Economics whom had been trusted with such a weapon for cutting the cake by Miss Morgenstern. Soon, large slices of melon were being eaten by all present and I had handed out the laboratory aprons which we used during experiments and I naturally for such an event I had donned my white coat. This had been a wise move as soon half-eaten pieces of water melon were sailing across the room, especially between Big Lazlo and some of the other boys in the room. A wholescale water melon fight had broken out with much laughter and general good nature.

Having eaten or expended all of the 'ammunition' the warring parties settled down to peaceful banter and some of the girls began to clean up the room. It was then that Big Lazlo, always keeping a tough exterior and some distance between himself and teachers quietly came up to the front bench and with a sheepish look handed me a brown paper bag. He gave me that 'you're one of us now

Ships' look and disappeared back to the anonymous crowd of boys at the rear bench. I took his farewell object out of the bag. It was a large, circular cigarette ash tray with decoration to make it look like an open toilet bowl as seen from above. In the centre of the 'bowl' a pleading face was looking up with the caption saying 'we don't swim in your toilet so don't p--- in our pool'. Obviously, it was meant for a smoker's poolside table. I had given up the smoking habit in second year College when pipe smoking had become the new rage with the incoming First Years, but this gift was the sort of object that Big Lazlo would consider the epitome of adult culture. I had hoped that his regular tobacconist would have given him a discount on such an item as a one of his preferred customers. Then again, it was probably obtained at no cost by slight of hand in the local cultural tourist shop.

So, I left West Capital High with many great memories and a heavy heart. I walked the last mile to the bus stop and waited the mandatory hour before taking its sad ride back to the city's centre. I said my farewells to Jacko and the gang that night knowing that I would not remember to do so later and that it would take me at least a day to recover after I went with them to the 'Rest' for a last few drink or more.

"Stupid bastard!" Jacko had said slapping me on the back and giving the best farewell comment he could muster. Will remained in his usual silent self and just smiled, giving me a knowing grin from a public servant who knew all about transferring from one department to another. I was going to miss that crowd and their crazy shenanigans which went on most weeks in the dark corridors of Capital House.

Several days and headaches later, I again caught a cab to the dismal railway station and caught the return National Capital Express back to Sydney. It proved to be just as slow as the one I had travelled in on my exited first trip from home. This time the trip would not be exciting but one of mixed feelings; mostly sadness. The water in the dusty old water carafes still sloshed back and forth and the old brown tendrils of brown flypaper still swayed in the breeze at each end of the carriage. I really hoped that the Wild Bunch, Butch Cassidy, Ned Kelly or some other train robber would leap onto the little balcony at the end of the carriage and yell 'this is a holdup' just to relieve my melancholy.

Still, I was going home and to a new school. I had already been accepted into the University for 'seven years hard with good behaviour' with experimental psychology and geology to be my First-Year subjects. My new school was well-known to me and going to be a very challenging learning curve in my career but very convenient for travel. Southside High had extended its curriculum past its 'Intermediate Technical' status and now went all the way to Year 12. I would be back into the traditional culture of survival of 'us versus them' with its detentions and canings, but I knew the character of the 'inmates' well enough and after all, I was now a man of experience.

About the Author

Dr. Peter Terence Scott was born in Sydney, Australia and had a professional teaching career spanning over forty years. In some regards, his career contained many of the events given in this book. Like Tom Shipley, he started his career as a two-year trained, junior secondary science teacher at age nineteen and learnt the lessons of his profession the hard way by experience. Later, he studied at university part time and obtained a Bachelor of Science degree whilst trying to carry on a normal life. Much later and inadvertently, he obtained Masters' Degrees in Science and Educational Administration and a Doctorate in Education. Involved in several government panels, including as Head of Curriculum, he was elected as a Teacher of the Year by an unsuspecting Government and retired to family life, traveling and writing books.

Other Books by the Author

FICTION

Letters from San Rafael (as Hernan Moreno Ruiz). Set in South America in the 1880's, this is a collection of letters smuggled home by Don Hernan Moreno, an Intelligence officer of the Peruvian Army who has been captured by the Ecuadorans during a border dispute. Taken to the fortified hacienda in Banos, in the mountains of Ecudor, he and his sargeant, Garcia, are treated as honoured guests. Each of the ten stories tells of the life and times of people in the hacienda and beyond. The final chapter is the climax of the entire book.

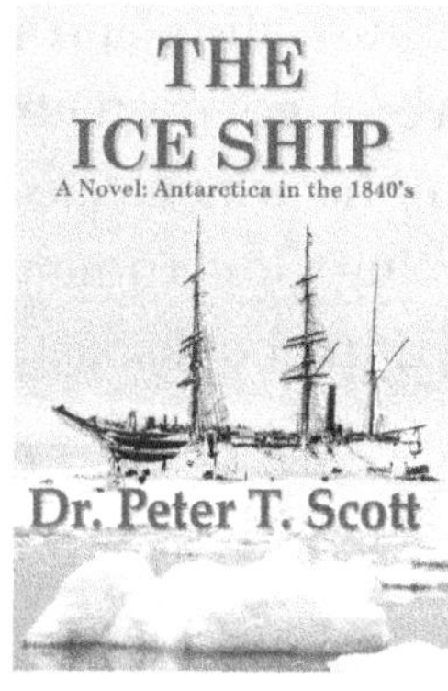

The Ice Ship. Set mainly in the Antarctic in the 1840's, this is the story of the survival of the crew of the futuristic auxiliary steam whaler, the AUSTRALIS which has become trapped in the ice following its voyage south along the Antarctic Peninsula. Based upon actual observations and experience of the author during a 2011 voyage into the same region on a small ex-research vessel.

NON-FICTION

Adventures in Earth Science is an in-depth, traditional Earth Science textbook on Geology, Meteorology, Oceanography and Astronomy. The latest scientific information has been given in the text including chapters on climate change and the future use of fuels and energy. The book contains over 700 pages, 1200 photographs and illustrations mostly taken by the author. It also includes 32 video links taken by the author to explain various skills as well as excursions to many exotic places in support of the text. Also has companion **Teachers' Guide** and **Laboratory Manual**.

The contents of this book have also been rearranged into the **Adventures in Earth Science Series** of eight smaller individual books in both electronic and A5 print editions.

| Exploration Science | Fossils- Life in the Rocks | Riches from the Earth | A Dangerous Planet: Volcanoes and Earthquakes |

Rocks - Building The Earth	Changing the Surface: Weathering And Erosion	Through Sea and Sky: Oceanography and Meteorology	Beyond Planet Earth: Astronomy

Adventures in Earth and Environmental Science is a two-volume textbook on the environment, how it is monitored and implications for the future. They come in electronic format and as A4-sized print editions with a **Laboratory Manual** for each volume and a **Teachers' Guide**.

Surviving Global Warming - A Guide for the Future is a comprehensive explanation of the natural and man-made causes of global warming with data from a wide range of reputable scientific bodies such as CSIRO and NASA. Written with many innovative suggestions for coping with the consequences of future global warming at the home, local and government levels. It comes as an electronic or printed edition.

All of these books are available in electronic format for any PC or tablet in Kindle format which can be read on any device using the free Kindle App. Or as print editions. Available at all Internet book outlets or from **Felix Publishing** by contacting them at:

info.felixpublishing@gmail.com

www.ingramcontent.com/pod-product-compliance
Lightning Source LLC
Chambersburg PA
CBHW070636170726
48291CB00003B/1032